THE ROMANY
HEIRESS

Other books by Nikki Poppen:

The Dowager's Wager
The Heroic Baron

THE ROMANY HEIRESS

•

Nikki Poppen

AVALON BOOKS
NEW YORK

Published by Thomas Bouregy & Co., Inc.
160 Madison Avenue, New York, NY 10016

Library of Congress Cataloging-in-Publication Data

Poppen, Nikki, 1967–
    The Romany heiress / Nikki Poppen.
        p. cm.
    ISBN 978-0-8034-9867-9 (acid-free paper)
    1. Nobility—Fiction. I. Title.

    PS3616.O657R66 2007
    813'.6—dc22

                                    2007024709

PRINTED IN THE UNITED STATES OF AMERICA
ON ACID-FREE PAPER
BY HADDON CRAFTSMEN, BLOOMSBURG, PENNSYLVANIA

For Catherine because you're so wild! I love to watch
you scream on roller coasters and dare your brother.
I hope you always embrace life fully like you do now.
This heroine is for you—she dances, she sings, she
gallops bareback on horses—a real daredevil like you.
But most importantly, she's kind and giving and has a
golden soul—just like you. I would walk the ends of
the earth for one of your hugs.

For Ellen H., who has read countless manuscript drafts
and believes they are all bestsellers. Every writer
needs a friend like her.

For my husband, the eternal hero. You see my dreams
and you make them possible. I can never overestimate
what you mean to our family.

I want to thank my agent at Greyhaus Literary Agency, Scott Eagen, for all his assistance. He has spent countless hours acting in the role of critic, agent, and publicist on behalf of this manuscript. He was there with me every step of the way from helping me clean up the manuscript to make it publisher-ready, selecting the right publishing house for this story (Avalon was right on the money, the perfect place), skillfully guiding me through the process of seeing a book published to being a diligent publicist, going above and beyond the call of the agent's duty.

Finally, thanks to my supportive P.E.O. chapter which has encouraged me every step of the way and always believed I would do this. I love all of you.

Prologue

*London, February 14, 1816, the alleyway
outside the Denbigh's townhouse, evening of the
Valentine masquerade*

In the alleyway behind the lavishly lit Mayfair mansion, Irina Dupeski tossed her dark curls and slipped out of the cheap, black cloak hiding the bright colors of her multihued skirt. She fluffed the full skirt and pinched her cheeks for effect. "How do I look?" She gave her companion a teasing smile and twirled once.

The muscular youth gave an adolescent stammer. "Irina, you look lovelier than ever." Then he puffed up his chest and offered in his best manly tone, "I should go with you. One can never tell what these lordlings might be like. You know as well as I do how the Rom are treated simply because we live outside of society. I do not want any of them to think you deserve less than a lady."

"I thank you for your worry, Jacopo, but it is not necessary. I have done performances like this for the *ton* before. I shall be safe. Remember, I will just be on the other side of the garden wall."

Jacopo cast a glance at the high bricked wall and grimaced. "I suppose I could climb it if it came to that."

Irina laughed. "I suppose you could but you could also use the gate." She reached up to test the latch of the gate, and it opened as planned. Giles, the man who had hired her, said he would arrange for it to be so. Jacopo, the darling, was still concerned. She reached a hand out to soothe the worry from his face. "This is nothing. I am telling fortunes for this Giles and a few of his friends. I won't be longer than a half hour. What could go wrong?"

Before he could answer, Irina slipped through the iron gate and into the town garden of the Denbigh's home. As expected, a heavily attended masquerade was well underway, evidenced by the noise and light spilling from the ballroom. She wished some of that light extended to the back of the garden. She could hardly see a foot in front of her. She didn't want to risk tripping over an errant root or snagging her skirts on an unseen bramble. She made her way forward, cautious and shivering. Without the protection of her cloak, there was no mistaking the bitter weather of winter, but she'd forgone the extra warmth for the sake of theatrics. She knew precisely the appeal she held for men when she was dressed in the full regalia of a gypsy fortune teller.

She needed every last crown and guinea she could wrest from this night's performance to add to her hidden stash in the floor of the wagon. The time was coming when she would leave the caravan and set out to claim her destiny. She might have lived all of her life to date as Rom but she would not die Rom. She would claim her rightful heritage and live the rest of her life as a lady, fulfilling the bedtime story that had been told to her since she was old enough to remember.

At last, after careful steps, Irina gained the verandah where Giles had asked her to meet his party of friends. There was no one present yet, but she'd planned on being deliberately early in order to become familiar with the setting. The area was wide, open, and cold. All the better for her safety, and all the better for getting the job done quickly. No doubt they would be as cold as she and would want to return to the warm crush of the ballroom.

Voices garnered her attention as the French doors leading from the ballroom flew open. She recognized the leader. Giles led the way, giving instructions over his shoulder. He caught sight of her and motioned her into the shadows with a quick wink.

Irina blended into the darkness and watched. She had forgotten how handsome Giles was with his deep-gold hair reminiscent of antiqued gold and his horseman's physique. As someone who'd spent her life traveling from one horse fair to another, she knew the difference instantly between a man who had pretensions of great horsemanship and a man who was born to the saddle. Giles was of the latter. From the width of his broad shoulders to the muscles of his thighs, he evinced superior skill with horses.

And with people, for that matter. He had never called himself by a title or a last name during their brief dealings, but she knew he was more than a mere mister by the clothes he wore and the manners he used. He didn't need to flaunt a title for her to know he was far above her in social standing, although he had treated her with gracious courtesy. She could not forget he was a member of high society and she was still Rom, at least for now, until she could make the fairy tale come true.

Irina smiled to herself in the shadows. She wouldn't always be Rom. Perhaps when she claimed her true inheritance, Giles might look her way. The fantasy of dancing with Giles warmed her chilled skin. She would wear a fine dress of aquamarine silk done in the latest fashion, with slippers and gloves to match. Around her neck would be a strand of freshwater pearls with mates at her ears. Perhaps she'd even have a strand wound through her upswept hair. Irina sighed, letting her imagination run rampant.

Then, all at once, it was show time. Giles gestured toward her with a gallant sweep of his extravagant, satin-lined cloak. Irina pushed her daydream to the back of her mind and stepped forward. She needed the coin from this evening if her dream was to become anything more. She curtsied and put on her best fabrication of a Russian accent, favoring Giles with a coy smile.

"These are your friends, milord?" She dimpled. "Ah, who shall be first?" she asked, dazzling each of the four assembled men with a practiced look and ignoring the one woman. While she tantalized, she studied them; the young blond lounging on the cold stone steps as if it were summer looked game enough and full of adventure. His fortune would be easy to tell; the lanky, black-haired man with obsidian eyes was easy enough to read as well. He was the quiet, bookish type, who hid his true ambitions; the other man present would not be so simple. He was sinfully handsome, and he wore his fine looks with an aura that suggested he knew just how a woman would be affected by one brooding glance. But he was brooding and not amused by the prospect of having his fortune read. She would save him for last, along with the lovely but tense woman who sat near him.

Crowd assessed, Irina began with the adventurous blond, caressing his palm and looking into his dancing green eyes. With each of them, she applied her trade ruthlessly. With the blond on the steps, she laughed and played the coy flirt, matching his remarks to her wit. With the quiet man she coaxed and rewarded, treating him as if he were the only man on the verandah. With the difficult one, she cajoled with all her talent until he reluctantly gave up his palm. With the woman she gave her truth, although it was obvious the woman was less than glad for it.

In the end, Irina knew she had done her job well. The group was laughing and satisfied with her efforts as they traded fortunes with one another. For a moment when they chuckled over their futures and included her in their teasing repartee, she felt like one of them, as if she belonged in just such a circle. But it was a moment too short-lived. It was with dismay that she let Giles lead her back into the shadows, discreetly escorting her down the verandah steps before anyone would notice she was gone.

What had she expected? That they invite her to join them? That one of the elegant gentlemen ask her dance or to go into supper with him? Of course not. She knew in their minds she was the hired help. No amount of talent or flirting would change that. At the end of the night, she would still be Rom.

Irina was keenly aware of Giles's hand at her back, guiding her effortlessly through the darkness. The stars twinkled overhead in the freezing night sky and for the brief walk Irina indulged herself, pretending this was her beau strolling her about a garden in full bloom at a spring fete. They might be off to find a secret place to steal a kiss. The gate loomed all too soon, and Giles was pressing a soft leather purse in her hand.

"Here's the payment we agreed upon. Thank you, Miss Dupeski. My friends enjoyed themselves immensely."

Miss Dupeski? Oh, this one had manners aplenty, treating her so politely. Irina cast him a glance through downcast eyes. She had read his fortune with the others on the steps, but she might entice him further. "My work is not yet done. Perhaps you would like a more extensive reading of your palm? Your true fortune remains to be told." She swept the area with a quick glance, spying a low stone bench half hidden by over-grown shrubs. "Allow me."

She led him to the bench and sank down on it, letting her skirts float in a rainbow as she settled, not that he could see the vibrant colors in the darkness of the gar-den. A smile quirked at his lips, and Irina knew he was mildly amused by her boldness, and maybe more.

She set to work, stroking the lines of his palm and murmuring to herself over what she saw.

"So, what else do you see?" he asked impatiently when she said nothing directly to him.

Irina looked up from the hand with carefully schooled features. This was the response she had been waiting for with her mutterings. It was a tried-and-true tactic for piquing the curiosity of even the most reluctant. He had been somewhat amused when she'd begun but she wanted him fully interested. "Somewhat amused" held no advantages for her. "Fully interested", well that held any number of opportunities.

"I see a man who has direction, who knows what he is about. You have plans and the determination to see them through," Irina began, feeling safe with her assumption. What man didn't have plans? Not all men were deter-mined but they thought they were, and no man liked to admit he wasn't. "You will face great challenges, but you will overcome them by maintaining your standards."

"That's it? What about love?" He asked when Irina relinquished his hand. "Everyone else's fortune dealt in romance. It seems wrong that mine would be devoid of it." He chuckled a little at his joke.

She smiled a little at that. Highborn or low, they were all the same in the end. She tilted her head in a practiced, pretty move meant to tease. "So it's love you want to know about?" She took his hand back into her own, this time studying the light calluses where his hand must curve about the reins in spite of wearing gloves. She traced the line running from his fourth finger and noticed he shivered slightly at the delicate contact. What a delightful piece of whimsy it was to think this gorgeous man was as affected by her as she was by him.

"This is your love line. Yours is long, which indicates a lifelong passion awaits you, although you will discover it when you least expect it." Safe enough. He could interpret that any way he liked.

Giles sighed. "I wish I could believe that."

The quiet of the night closed around them. In the midst of his confession, Irina forgot she was cold, forgot their differences in station. "Why do you say that? Surely a man of your great appeal will find a woman." She breathed, not daring to break the spell that wove about them.

"I have no doubt I will find a woman. I do doubt I will find one that sparks a great passion in me. My father certainly didn't. Passionate liaisons don't run in our blood." He gave a rueful look that said he was half serious, half mocking in his admission.

Silence stretched between them as they held one another's gaze. Irina's heart pounded with expectation. He was going to kiss her. She could see the idea of the action forming in his striking blue eyes. At the last moment he rose from the bench, brushed at his evening pants, and offered her his arm. "I fear I've kept you overlong, Miss Dupeski. I hope someone is waiting at the gate to see you home. If not, I'll arrange . . ."

Irina interrupted swiftly, smarting from the disappointment there would be no kiss. "There is no need. My friend, Jacopo, is there. I will be safe."

"Very well, then," Giles said with stiff politeness, holding the narrow gate open for her. Irina brushed by him, conscious of her skirts sweeping his legs and the spiced cleanliness of his scent as she passed. A queer flutter ran through her. Her mentor, Magda, would call it a premonition. This would not be the last time she saw Giles, although she had no reason to believe why it would be so. They obviously did not run in the same social circles, and he had given no indication that he would seek her out after this evening.

Irina looked back only once as Jacopo slipped the welcome warmth of her cloak about her shoulders. She gave a small wave to let Giles know she was safe. His duty was discharged. He could return to his friends and the party. Someday she would be like them. Someday she wouldn't have to feign a Russian accent or keep up the pretense of telling fortunes.

She said little to Jacopo on the way back to the caravan, too lost in her thoughts about Giles to do more than offer cursory comments to his questions about the mansion and the rich people inside.

Back at the caravan on the outskirts of London she tried to describe her feelings to Magda while she sipped hot coffee inside the *vardo*, glad to be warm again.

Magda gave a mirthless laugh, which Irina did not find reassuring. "My dear, what you're feeling is akin to having a ghost walk over your grave. Tonight you've meddled with fate."

"What do you mean?" Irina asked over the rim of her chipped cup. She was not given to superstitions like Magda and the others in the caravan but still, Magda's words sent a chill through her.

"I mean exactly what I say." The older woman retorted. "What was the name of your young man?"

"Giles."

"Just Giles? No last name? No title?"

"No."

"Very well, it is enough. Your young man is Giles Moncrief. He's the heir to Spelthorne Abbey."

Irina spluttered, spewing a mouthful of coffee. "Spelthorne? He's the earl?"

"He *will* be the earl." Magda corrected. "The man who will stand between you and your rightful inheritance."

"But Spelthorne is mine," Irina protested. "I have the birth certificate and the diary. I thought there was no heir but me."

"There is no *legitimate* heir but you. Did you expect to walk up to Spelthorne and find it unoccupied? Did you expect to claim it without a fight?" Magda scolded her naivety. Her middle-aged features hardened. "To

claim it, you will have to fight him for it, but not yet."
Magda waved a long finger in warning. "You have met
your fate too soon. It is not time. He is not yet earl. To
expose yourself while the old earl yet lives is to weaken
your claim. We must leave in morning. We dare not risk
another encounter."

Magda rose and busied herself with her shawls. "I'll
explain it all to Tommasino. He is a good leader, and
he'll understand our need for haste."

Magda vanished out the door before Irina could
question her further. She was aghast at the news. Giles
was a Spelthorne? Every fantasy she'd entertained that
evening fractured into a thousand pieces. If she won
her heart's desire, he would never look her direction
with anything other than hatred for what she had done
to him.

Her conscience chided her for such weakness. A
handsome face was not near enough reason to forego
the legacy she had waited years to claim. Since she was
old enough to understand, Magda had tucked her into
bed with the story—the tale that she was an earl's
daughter, traded at birth for a cottager's son simply because the peer desired a male heir.

At first, she had thought the story nothing more than
a common child's fairy tale. After all, what child
doesn't entertain notions that he or she is a prince or
princess in hiding? As the years progressed, Magda
embellished the account with more details as she became old enough to understand them. Details such as
the name of the holding, the name of the earl and his

wife, descriptions of the house, its floor plan and its grounds until Irina could see the place in her mind with alarming clarity although the caravan had never been there during her own lifetime. According to Magda, the last time the caravan had camped at Spelthorne was the September of her birth. Magda had been there, assisting her mother, when the deal had been made.

Finally, on her twentieth birthday, Magda had produced the most significant details—a diary written by her mother, Celeste Moncrief, the Countess of Spelthorne, and a birth certificate.

Irina had stared at the birth certificate, speechless and shattered. 'You've got the wrong girl,' she'd whispered horrified. The name on the birth certificate wasn't hers. The certificate belonged to a Catherine Celeste Moncrief. Long moments passed before she realized the import of it. She wasn't Caterina, affectionately called Irina by those in the caravan, *she* was Catherine.

The enormity of it had been overwhelming. She was Catherine Moncrief, a child switched at birth, switched from a life of comfort into a life of struggle and stigmatism, switched into anonymity where not even her name was her own. She had been angry for days. She'd wanted to march straight to Spelthorne Abbey and throw down the proverbial gauntlet. But Magda had said simply, "not yet" and she had not questioned the wise woman's advice.

Now, eight years later, she was still waiting. Now, Magda no longer said "not yet," she said "soon." Her time was coming. That scared her. She hoped she had the strength to do what was demanded of her. Her success would cause the ruin of an innocent man who was intricately woven into the scheme that had duped her of her heritage.

Irina sighed. When she had forecasted great challenges in his life that evening she had done so generically. All lives had challenges but she had not expected she would be one of his.

Chapter One

Two years later, Spelthorne Abbey, Northern Surrey England, mid-September 1818

Giles Moncrief stood on the wide verandah of Spelthorne Abbey, his family estate, and flipped open the simple but expensive gold pocket watch he carried. It was 4:00 according to the hands of his watch face. But he hadn't needed to open the watch to know that. The appearance of men newly returned and washed from a day of well-planned fishing on the River Ash, milling about with their wives beneath the white canopies dotting the lawn and the arrival of tea indicated the time of day just assuredly as any clock. His house parties always ran on schedule. Always.

By rights, he should be elated the party was going so well. The weather had cooperated with blue skies. The light breeze coming in off the river contrived to keep the guests comfortable in the last throes of summer. The horse fair a few miles away in Staines would provide entertainment tomorrow, allowing his guests to get out of the house and into the glorious Surrey countryside. His personal *coup de grace* was the presence of his closest friends, Alain Hartsfield, the Baron Wickham and Tristan Moreland, the Viscount Gresham, along with their wives. The collection of close friends hadn't seen each other for awhile, making the party a reunion of sorts for them.

Giles surveyed all that lay before him, waiting to be filled with the usual satisfaction he experienced from orchestrating such flawless occasions. Today that sense of pleasure was strangely absent. Not even the presence of Lady Fox-Haughton, his current but discreet *affaire de coeur*, could vanquish the emptiness that filled him despite all that surrounded him.

Down on the lawn, Alain waved up at him and beckoned for him to join them. Giles smiled and waved back in affirmation.

Giles wended his way toward them through the canopies set up on the vast west lawns of Spelthorne Abbey, under which resided tables and chairs for tea and blankets thrown about picnic-style for the younger or more adventurous guests.

Laughter reigned at the canopy claimed by Alain and Tristan, their wives, and little Alain-Alexander, Tristan and Isabella's son. Tristan clapped Giles on the back good-naturedly. "Finally, we get you to ourselves. You've been so busy playing host."

Giles smiled and rocked back on his heels, quick humor on his lips. "These parties don't happen by accident," he joked.

Isabella spoke up from her haphazard couch of pillows. "Of course not, and no one is better at organizing such events than you," she enthused, careful to keep an ever-watchful eye on her toddling eighteen-month-old son.

"I will tell cook that her efforts were well-received. She will appreciate the compliment." Giles made a half bow in her direction. To his eye, Isabella looked lovely in her casual repose. With her honey-colored hair and tawny eyes, Isabella had been born to great beauty, but marriage to Tristan and motherhood had increased her beauty tenfold. Giles suspected it was due to the contentment she had found with the enigmatic viscount. The ache of emptiness he had experienced earlier flared again.

A sudden movement on the blanket drew Giles' attention. Alain-Alexander had succeeded in escaping his mother's reach and was attempting to stuff the remaining lemon scones in his mouth. In a swift movement, Tristan bent down and scooped the little boy up unto his broad shoulders while the little boy laughed and dropped crumbs in Tristan's hair.

"One scone is enough for you, little man, or you'll end up with a stomachache tonight," Tristan admonished playfully. He tossed the little boy up in the air, catching him and tickling him when he came down.

Giles thought the boy liked it immensely, if the whoops he made were any indication.

"Tristan! Your roughhousing is what will give him the stomachache." Isabella scolded, reaching to take Alain-Alexander and settle him back on her lap. A soft, knowing smile passed between the couple as Tristan relinquished the boy.

Another queer pang tightened in his belly as Giles watched the familial scene unfold. He cast a covert glance and caught Alain exchanging a quiet smile with his wife, Cecile. A discreet hand slipped briefly to her waist. Ah, there would be another happy announcement among their circle of friends soon.

He did not begrudge his friends their happiness. But Giles could not deny the tinge of sadness he felt when he saw them together with their families. For the first time in the seventeen years he, Alain, and Tristan had been friends, he felt a chasm between him and them.

Over the last few years, Alain and Tristan had had adventures of their own of which he had not been part. Tristan had served in the British fight against Napoleon as a covert agent. Alain had dedicated himself to single-handedly bringing oppressed French citizens to safety in England. They had had their adventures; they had found their true loves. They were bringing children into the world.

All at once, the source of his ache became clear. He was not being left out—indeed, he stood as godfather to young Alain-Alexander—he was being left behind.

"Giles, you're wool-gathering." Alain remarked. "Tristan just asked about the evening's entertainment. Many of us were speculating on it down at the river this afternoon."

"Ah, my apologies," Giles said glibly, covering his inattention. "Tonight's entertainment is a secret." He dropped his voice conspiratorially, "I've hired a troop of performers, acrobats, jugglers and the like. In fact, right now, my footmen are no doubt setting up the performing area on the south garden lawn."

"What's an acwrobat?" Alain-Alexander bounced excitedly on Tristan's shoulders as he tried out the new word.

Giles gave the little boy a smile and reached out to tickle his foot. "An acrobat is someone who does tricks with his body, like turning circles in the air." Giles winked. "Can you keep a secret young man?" When the boy nodded, Giles went on, "There's to be a fireworks display afterwards."

The boy's eyes grew big. "Can I stay up, daddy?"

"Now you've done it, Giles. You have gone and spoiled him. How can I say no to that?" Tristan grinned up at the boy.

"I'm his godfather. It's my job. Now, if you will excuse me, I think I will take a walk before dinner and enjoy some much earned solitude." Giles said with a joviality he did not feel.

A walk would clear his head and let him sort through the revelations racing through it. Away from the demands of the party, he could put his thoughts in order and gain a perspective on his current situation.

He chose his favorite path, a bridle trail that ran along the creek to the north of the property. The trail would loop back to bring him up on the south side by the gardens where the evening festivities would take place.

Already the burble of the creek and the shade of the trees soothed him. He breathed deeply of the summer scents of the forest around him. How he loved this land! The abbey and its extensive grounds had never failed to thrill him, to fire his blood, to define his purpose. Strolling under the green-leafed bounty of the summer trees was a potent reminder that he had been born to this land, born to be the Earl of Spelthorne.

His whole life had revolved around becoming Spelthorne. When his father died two years ago, Giles had been ready to take up an earl's considerable responsibilities with his trademark competence.

How could he doubt the direction of his life when it had followed its pre-ordained course and achieved the desired results? He was master of the place he loved most in the world. He nurtured it, protected it, like a parent does a beloved child. His mind veered in that direction.

Children. Eventually there would be children here to take up the banner of Spelthorne's legacy. Giles knew that with certainty. Just as all else had followed in due time in his well-ordered life, so would the taking of an appropriate wife and the getting of heirs.

Giles stopped and skipped a handful of pebbles in the stream. The serenity he coveted slipped away at the notion of setting up his nursery. Family and a spouse should have reassured him. The thought of acquiring a dutiful wife, as well versed in duty and order as himself, did not fill him with satisfaction. Watching Tristan and Isabella, and Alain and Cecile, he knew more than compatibility in marriage was possible. His friends had all managed to find great passion as well.

He had been promised a great passion once upon a time. Unbidden, the lovely fortune-teller's prediction came to mind. She'd spoken of overcoming challenges and finding passion. For a moment in that bleak garden he had thrilled to her words, feeling like a conquering knight of old at the thought of facing down challenges and claiming a lady fair for his own. Then she'd slipped through the gate and into the night. The moment passed, and he became Giles Moncrief the unexceptional again.

He should have acted on his impulses that night. He should have given his hands the free rein they ached for and let them run through the silky darkness of her hair. He should have gathered her to him and kissed her soundly on the full, inviting lips of her luscious red mouth. Even now, his body roused to his mind's image of her perched on the low bench, hair tossed back, skirts swirling about her, her sharp green eyes studying him, not quite able to hide the reckless streak within and promising him the chance at a great passion.

Giles threw the last pebble forcefully, hoping to

exorcise the potent memory. Well, there was still time for his fortune to come true. Anything could happen. Of course, he didn't really expect it to. Nothing simply "happened" to a man who did not make a habit of living life spontaneously. He was not Tristan or Alain, whose penchant for adventure had catapulted them down several unplanned avenues in their day. He was the Earl of Spelthorne. At the age of thirty-one, he had achieved his life's desire. That should be enough. He should not wish for more. Many men lived entire lives achieving less.

Giles clung to that thought, repeating it like a mantra until the south lawn came into view. Down on the grass, activity reigned. His footmen were setting up a wide, raised platform for the performers. In a different section of the lawn, finishing details were underway on the white-clothed tables where the guests would dine alfresco amid his prized flowers and summer candlelight.

Giles drew a deep, steadying breath. Yes, this should be enough for any man. Armed with that fortifying knowledge, he strode toward the activity to see what had transpired during his short absence.

What had looked like organized activity from his vantage point looked more like chaos close-up. As soon as he neared the stage, Giles knew something was wrong. A brightly painted gypsy *vardo* was parked behind the stage and a dark-haired woman dressed in deep purple skirts stood toe to toe with the footman Giles had left in charge.

An argument was in progress by the time Giles was within earshot and growing more ridiculous by the moment given that the woman couldn't have been more than three inches over five feet and his footman was a robust six foot if not a bit more—a point that was heavily emphasized by their proximity to one another. His footman should know better. The first rule of any encounter was discretion. The pair was beginning to draw a crowd.

With practiced ease, Giles clapped a strong hand on the footman's shoulder. "Reginald, what is the problem here?"

"My lord, forgive me. This gypsy claims to be the entertainment you've hired for this evening. I told her you were expecting the acting troupe from Staines to travel over for the entertainments." His tone carried a hint of superiority as he laid out his information, obviously expecting his answer to be collaborated.

"That is correct." Giles agreed, noting that the affirmation brought a near sneer of victory to Reginald's face. He would have to remind Reginald that one did not gloat in the face of the defeated. Rule two of any encounter was to claim victory with humility. No one liked a conceited winner. It made for future antagonism and enemies.

"Gentlemen, if I may have a moment to explain the circumstances before you decide between yourselves to have us thrown off the property without hearing all the evidence?" The woman said in a tone that indicated her displeasure over being treated as invisible.

Giles turned to the woman, taking her in for the first

time since he'd come down the slope. The world stopped. The bustle around him faded into a dull whir and nothing mattered but the apparition before him, conjured directly from his ruminations at the creek. Midnight curls spilled to her waist. Jade-colored eyes sparked with the thrill of the fight. High cheek bones added an aristocratic element to her face that was tempered by the fullness of cherry lips. If the Snow White of children's tales came to life, she was this woman incarnate.

Only this woman was more sensual, more mature than any child's princess, and much more to his liking. He'd never given much attention to the young debutantes that flooded London every spring. His tastes ran to the more sophisticated woman.

There was no mistaking that she was a vision from his past, the one fantasy he'd allowed himself. The woman was undeniably Irina Dupeski.

For the sake of maintaining good form in front of the servants, he could not admit he knew her. For the sake of not looking like a foolish school boy who couldn't control his body, he could not give away the effect she was having on him.

Giles crossed his arms over his chest and said in his best authoritative tones, "My man is right. You are not the people I hired."

She gave him a long stare that belied her recognition of him. "Spelthorne?"

"I am." Giles held her gaze, somewhat mollified that she shared some shock as well at seeing him again. It was gratifying that she remembered him. Still, he found himself willing her not to say anything about their previous association, as innocent as it was.

"My man is right. You are not the troupe I hired. I suggest you explain yourself."

"The acting troupe has eaten tainted food and is unable to perform tonight. We have offered to come in their place," she said simply, her gaze never leaving his.

Giles gave a cold smile, the romanticism he'd felt earlier disappearing in the face of reality. Along with her beauty, he now recalled how well she'd worked his friends that night on the verandah—flirting with Alain, teasing Chatham, and coaxing Tristan.

At the time, he'd been mesmerized by her efforts, finding her behavior simply vivacious. But later, goaded by Isabella's skepticism over the event, he'd wondered if it had all been calculated persuasion on Irina's part. Making him and his friends happy would certainly be more profitable than disappointing them. She was probably working him now, in an attempt to grab a quick purse. She would find he was no country simpleton.

"I see. How commendable that you should perform in their place. I suppose the size of the promised purse or the opportunity to enchant an audience of peers had no impact on your decision? Tell me, did you pay the innkeeper to feed them tainted food or did you simply sour it yourself?" His logical mind was comfortable with such an approach. His heart was not. It preferred to remember the tender chemistry that had sprung between them on the stone bench when no one had been around to see. It preferred to believe neither of them had been acting then.

She bristled at the accusation, color rising gloriously in her cheeks. "How dare you make such assumptions!"

"How dare you assume I can be fooled." Giles ground out, holding to his logical line. "Remove your *vardo* and your companions at once, and I won't involve the law."

The woman did not budge. "If we leave you won't have entertainment for the evening. Regardless of the methods involved, the troupe is not going to perform. It is us or no one, milord."

Giles noted she did not deny his charges of trickery further.

She tossed her black curls and cocked her head in a pretty gesture Giles remembered. "Call a truce, milord, you cannot prove your claims nor can I prove my innocence. We'll take your pay. You'll take our services, and the *vardo* will be gone in the morning."

In the distance the dressing bell for dinner sounded at the house. The green-eyed minx had him at a disadvantage. He had no time to engineer a counter plan for the evening's entertainment.

Giles gave a curt nod. "We are agreed." *Especially the "gone in the morning" part.* Irina Dupeski with her tantalizing beauty and shrewd ways was a dangerous combination.

As the evening went on, Giles' concerns took a new avenue. The dinner was spectacular under the summer stars; Cook having outdone herself with the stuffed duck in aspic and the tender summer asparagus covered lightly with cream sauce. The gypsy troupe amused his guests with juggling, comic skits, dancing, and music.

It was only when it was time for the fireworks, signaling the evening's finale, Giles realized Irina hadn't made an appearance. He had not caught sight of her in any of the acts. Her absence left him uneasy. *What was she up to?* It was too simple to assume she'd been unnerved by their encounter and left. No, she was here somewhere.

The prospect of ferreting out Irina Dupeski filled him with an awkward mix of excitement and anxiety. Further encounters with the Rom beauty could serve no practical purpose. He could not pursue her. She was not of his social class, and he was far too responsible when it came to relationships with women to engage in the only sordid option available to him where Irina was concerned. Besides, based on their heated exchange on the lawn, it was not even clear that she held that kind of interest in him.

The crowd oohed and aahed over the pyrotechnics that arched over the lake and the summer house visible in the distance from the lawn. Lady Fox-Haughton squeezed his arm under the cover of darkness, as the last of the show faded from the sky. "Giles, you're a genius. People will talk about this party for ages." She gushed, elegant and proud to be at his side during his moment of triumph.

He accepted her congratulations with a benign smile that masked his inner turmoil and dismissed her as politely as possible. He had no appetite for what she offered tonight.

Finally, having seen all his guests settled for the evening and bidding goodnight to Tristan and Alain, Giles climbed the stairs, eager for the solitude of his chambers where he could decide what to do about Irina's absence. He was torn between giving into the temptation of going to find her and the rational choice of staying safely ensconced in his rooms until the *vardo* was gone and Irina was out of his life once more.

Giles stepped inside his chambers and stilled. The lamp his valet usually left burning low was turned up high, illuminating the room and the obvious fact that he was not alone.

The object of his unrest sat in the overstuffed chair by the open window, her feet tucked beneath her skirts and her attention claimed by the book which lay open in her lap. She looked utterly beautiful with the lamplight catching the dark hues of her hair and accenting the gentle curve of her jaw.

For a moment Giles could only stare. *What would it be like to have such a woman waiting every night?* He was a man of culture and breeding, unaccustomed to primal instinct, but the need to possess and protect surged through him at the sight of her. She turned the page of her book, unaware of his presence.

"Can you read?" Giles asked. He had not meant to speak the thought out loud.

She startled at the sound of his voice, snapping the book shut and glared. "Yes, I can read. Not all gypsies are illiterate. Does that surprise you?" She was hard and cold, much like she'd been on the lawn. The vision of gentle femininity evaporated.

Dismayed by the shattered vision, Giles matched her cold hauteur. "What surprises me is finding an uninvited woman in my rooms. I am tired and have a long day of entertaining ahead of me tomorrow."

She rose to her feet in a fluid movement, her coldness melting, and a soft smile on her lips that restored Giles's earlier image of gentle tranquility. She moved toward him, hips swaying as she closed the remaining distance between them. He was bewitched. It was much harder to resist the lovely siren that stood before him than the shrew-tongued gypsy from the lawns.

"We have not gotten off to a good start. I am sorry about the scene on the lawn. It was a shock seeing you again." She said softly, sincerely.

She was close enough for Giles to smell the delicate scent of lavender that clung to her skin, to notice the pulse that beat at the base of her neck, exposed by the cut of her white blouse. He furrowed his brow. Her pulse seemed slightly elevated as if she were nervous or distressed. It was at odds with the soothing quality of her voice, her soft demeanor.

Unless it was all an act.

Giles found the strength to resist her calculated allure and scolded himself for nearly giving in. He was back on guard. "What do you want?"

He could see she was surprised by his tone. She'd thought she had him.

"I need to speak with you, privately, Giles. There is business between us that needs settling."

"I paid the wagon driver. Our business is settled," Giles said tersely.

She shook her head, the dark ringlets swaying at the motion. She slipped a hand into the billowy bodice of her blouse, and for a moment Giles thought he knew exactly what kind of "business" she referred to. Was she going to seduce him?

She brought out a slim leather folder, the kind used for legal documents. She handed it to him.

"What is this?" Giles asked, turning the folder over in his hands and redirecting his thoughts. A cold chill passed through him. He knew instinctively the folder held no good for him.

Irina squared her shoulders and lifted her chin to meet his gaze evenly. Her voice was quiet and firm. "It is my claim to Spelthorne as its legitimate heir."

Chapter Two

She'd expected any other man to bluster and rage upon hearing her news. To his credit, Spelthorne did not. Years of genteel training were evident in his controlled response.

"These are very serious accusations." The Earl of Spelthorne's intense blue gaze never wavered. He crossed his arms in a formidable gesture Irina was getting all too used to recognizing. Arms, she noticed, that bulged at the seams of his expensively tailored evening coat.

Under his scrutiny, the enormity of her contentions threatened to swamp her as she gathered her reserves to unswervingly answer his stare, all the while quailing inside. He was right. Such claims would not be treated lightly by him or by peerage.

For the first time since she embarked on this course,

she doubted her ability to see it through. What was she doing, challenging the well-connected and highly eligible Earl of Spelthorne? If she gave up now, there was still a chance she could meekly walk away and abandon her cause. No matter that the onus of truth was on her side, the earl was far beyond her reach. She did not doubt he could uphold his threats.

A man like him would indeed drag her through every court in the land. He'd have the peerage and years of presumption on his side. He could easily outlast her defense and pile of hardearned coins. But she had reason to believe it wouldn't come to that. For that reason, she stayed.

She had known from the outset that a man such as Giles would fight to the death to keep what was his—or in this case—what he thought was his. She'd known since meeting him that he was a man dedicated to his responsibilities and a man of unimpeachable honor. But she also knew such traits were a double-edged sword. She was counting on that sword cutting both ways.

Neither would Giles renounce the abbey and his title without a protracted fight, nor would he turn her away without recompense if he could be persuaded to believe her claim. She might not get the abbey or the title of lady, but she'd get enough to ensure she didn't have to spend her life traveling the countryside in a *vardo*, suffering lusty looks from men who thought she could be had simply because she was Rom.

Irina stopped her thoughts right there to steel herself. She would *not* be intimidated into a compromise because the man standing before her was beautifully made, dressed in fine clothes and possessed of a stare so penetrating it suggested he could divine all her thoughts and insecurities. She squelched the notion. It was too dangerous. If she started thinking all she'd get from him was a financial settlement akin to nothing more than hush money, then indeed that was all she could expect.

She'd waited her whole life for more than that. Money could be spent. She wanted a title. She wanted to be a lady and it was her due by birth. She did nothing wrong in laying claim to her birthright. It was unfortunate that her birthright had to be in the possession of a man so handsome that a simple glance at him conjured up butterflies in her stomach.

The earl cleared his throat. "If you would kindly leave, I will forget this ridiculous hoax you are attempting to perpetrate."

His air of superiority caused something to snap inside Irina. With that condescending attitude he was suddenly less than handsome. It lent her the courage she needed. She had not come here to be dismissed out of hand like an errant beggar on the back stoop or worse, a twopenny con artist.

"You haven't even opened the folder." She flicked her eyes to the leather case he held in his hands. "There is proof inside that I am who I say I am."

He raised his eyebrows, conveying his skepticism without uttering a word. He took the chair across from the one she'd occupied and crossed his booted legs at the heels, affecting a pose of leisure. "Shall I guess what is inside? Is it a birth certificate? A will naming you heir?"

Irina schooled her features to give nothing away. She realized he was mocking the very items which had sustained her hopes over the long years. She grabbed the folder from him when it became obvious he had no intentions of opening it. She pulled out the document concealed inside and pressed it flat on the table between the two chairs. "This is a copy of my birth certificate. It shows that I am the daughter of Celeste and George Moncrief, Earl and Countess of Spelthorne, born September 14, 1787."

If she had thought to win points in her favor for this disclosure, she would be disappointed. The earl looked at the paper and sighed indulgently, his tone still mocking. "My dear, you shall have to do far better than this. This paper is the kind of forgery sold on the London streets every day. I hope you haven't squandered a great sum on this."

"I have spent nothing on it," Irina pressed. "It is notarized by the village curate here in Spelthorne and signed by the doctor, William Tallbridge. I doubt a common forgery would produce those details."

"A forger could do so if you provided the names. Besides, I have nothing against which to match the signatures of the witnesses. For your convenience, or inconvenience depending on how you look at it, Dr. Tallbridge passed on last winter and the curate was promoted years ago to his own parish. Neither is here to serve as your witnesses." The earl countered smugly, tucking his arms behind his head as he stretched in the chair. Irina almost believed he was enjoying himself.

She fought the urge to bite her lip in frustration. Those circumstances were unfortunate. She'd not been able to ascertain the whereabouts of the two witnesses. She'd merely hoped one of them would still be about. After all, life didn't change quickly or often in the country.

She persisted. "This is not a forgery. It was given to me by the woman who accompanied me into exile and was present at my birth."

The earl laughed out loud at that. "Is she dead too? Does it bother you that all who hold the key to ensuring the success of your charade are gone? Even the supposed parents are both deceased. There is no one to believe your papers or support your claims." His tone became irritatingly deferential as he rose and began pacing. "You've had your laugh. Your little scam is not going to play well here. If noblemen gave into such claims every time a bastard by-blow issued a declaration of legitimacy the peerage would be in constant turmoil. I will thank you to take your papers and get out. Your claim to be a sister of sorts is summarily dismissed and as such any claim you might have to my home."

Irina rose to meet him, her voice quiet with its force. "You don't understand. I don't claim to be your sister by any stretch of blood. Indeed, my lord, I don't claim to be any relation at all seeing as you are nothing more than a cottager's son bought for a bag of guineas by a woman who would ensure that her husband had a male heir at all costs."

"You go too far!" Spelthorne whirled on her with an unrestrained roar.

He was magnificent in his anger, and she was gratified to note that at last she'd gotten past his well-
polished exterior. She drew a battered red book from a
hidden pocket in her skirts. "It's all written here in Celeste's journal." She held it out to him.

The earl seemed to blanch at the evidence and then
recovered his bravado. "Again, without collaboration,
written proof is easy enough to forge. There is no one
to support what you say."

"No one but you, Spelthorne." She made her ultima-
tum. "Search your heart. You know the truth regarding
the nature of your parents' relationship. You will know
whether or not what is inside the journal is the truth.
There are things in the journal no one would know;
things no one could find out years later and fabricate.
Read it, and you'll know for certain."

The earl's dashing blue eyes narrowed. "You should
know that I will not be compelled to give testimony
against myself. I will not cede this place or title to anyone. This place is mine by the burden of responsibility,
if nothing else."

"And it is mine by blood. I was born to it." Irina retorted, rising to the fight. "I will not be fobbed off."

The handsome earl smiled and nodded smugly, the
anger dissipating in the wake of his knowing grin. Irina
felt her knees turn watery beneath the heavy folds of
her skirts. It wouldn't do for him to know how affected
she was by a smile. If he knew, he would simply kiss
her into dropping her claim. She blushed at the image
conjured by her thoughts. She'd heard of women who

had traded away sensible options for a few moments of stolen pleasure. She would not be one of them, not after coming so far and risking so much. Tonight she was alone in the world except for the small trunk she'd stashed under Giles's bed and the coins hidden inside, scrimped together from years of hard work.

"Everyone has their price. What is yours?"

It wasn't until she processed his words that she realized how dangerously far afield her thoughts had wandered and why he was smiling. He smiled because he was attempting to buy her. Well, the price might be more than he was willing to pay.

"I want to stay at the abbey until you've read the diary and have reached your conclusions, whatever they might be, about my claims."

The request won her the startled look she sought. "What? No request for a thousand pounds or a townhouse in London and an annual allowance? Do you think your price is wise? I shall read the diary during the remainder of the night, and I shall conclude against you by morning. I will send you off with a hearty breakfast and that shall be the end."

"You say that only because you haven't read the diary yet."

"You are a fool to think I can be so easily gulled. Regardless of what the diary says, I won't concede Spelthorne to you." Spelthorne argued.

The lamp burned low, having used its reserve of oil, casting shadows in the ever-darkening room. Irina stepped forward, closer to Spelthorne. Perhaps it was time to change tactics. She doubted there was any headway to be made arguing logic with a man who was both intelligent and used to getting his own way. She dared to rest a hand on the starched perfection of his white shirt, reveling in the feel of the strong chest beneath, even as it reminded her that she toyed with a man powerful in all ways. Her voice was low and husky when she spoke.

"Yes, you will. I know you, Giles Moncrief. You are a man of honor. You would not tolerate your life being built on a wrong done to another."

"You know nothing about me." His voice echoed the husky tones of hers, his eyes drawn to the heat of her hand where it pressed against him and she knew a small victory. Her breath caught at the realization. This man was drawn to her. Magda would tell her to use that against him but her own moral code, so different than that of the Rom, did not find the option appealing.

Still, she could not step back from seizing the moment. "You are a man of honor and great passion." She whispered, lifting her eyes to his, unprepared for the blue fire that blazed within them.

"Yes, so you told me once. But that fortune has not come to pass. You promised me a great passion but I have yet to find it." The dangerous glint in his eyes confirmed he knew the proverbial battlefield was shifting from logic to something else.

Who was flirting with whom now? She would have to remind him she was doing the flirting here. Irina traced a line down his chest with a light finger. She tipped her head backward, letting her train of curls fall down her back while she looked up at him. "Haven't you?"

Desire kindled plainly in his eyes at her suggestion. She whetted her lips in invitation. To make sure there was no room for misunderstanding, she stepped into him, feeling the lightest brush of his lips on hers, catching the scent of wine on his breath, reminiscent of his elaborate dinner. She fell into the kiss, letting Giles's arms take her weight—only they didn't.

A man coughed, and then she was falling in an ignominious heap to the floor.

"Excuse me, Giles." A smooth voice said from the doorway unbothered by what he'd interrupted.

Irina noted it took Giles a moment to gather himself. It was small satisfaction though when her ankle throbbed from landing on it. The blackguard had dropped her.

"Tristan, what can I do for you?"

The dark viscount lounged dangerously in the doorway, a laugh hovering about his mouth. "I think the better question is what I can do for you. Is everything alright? I have the room next door. I thought I heard a heated argument." He raised a challenging eyebrow, daring any one to contradict his assumptions.

Irina felt her skin heat. Who knew what else he guessed at? She was thankful at least for the dim light which hid the worst of her flush. What awful luck that Giles's dear friend was next door. She didn't miss the implications of that. The viscount had made it subtly clear that he would not tolerate his friend being taken advantage of.

In her mortification, Irina wanted to shout her virtue out loud. She had dared a kiss, nothing more.

"Ahem, Catherine?" Giles looked down at her and offered her a hand up. "Shall we get you settled? I am sure you're tired from your delayed journey. I'll have your trunk sent to the east wing. There's a room for you there." He toed the part of the trunk peeping out from under his bed. "It seems the footmen brought it to the wrong room."

The use of her birthname startled her but she saw the rationale for it. Tristan might recall her from the long ago night on the Denbigh's porch. She was not ready to voice her claims to Giles's friends. Silently, she thanked Giles for the kindness.

A footman arrived, grumpy from being awakened in the middle of the night and took her trunk. She had no choice but to follow it to her room, wherever the west wing was. But she left feeling victorious. She'd won round one. Giles had accepted the wager. He would read the diary.

Giles stood rigidly, watching Irina/Catherine disappear down the hall. He waited. Tristan would have something to say. He wouldn't have so flagrantly violated protocol by bursting into his chambers if there hadn't been cause.

"*That* is not Lady Fox-Haughton," Tristan offered by way of observation, as Irina faded down the hallway.

"No. It is not," Giles said stiffly.

"When you said there would be fireworks tonight, I thought you'd meant pyrotechnics. I didn't think it would be your seducing the gypsy queen from the *vardo*."

"Don't be crass, Tristan." Giles raked his hands through his hair.

"You've always been a cut above such behavior, is all." Tristan shrugged.

Giles turned towards the window and sighed. There was no shaking Tristan when he was on to something. For whatever reason, Tristan smelled blood now. He wouldn't get his friend out of his room until Tristan had heard the whole story. "She claims to be the only legitimate child from my parents' marriage." Giles gestured towards the documents spread on the table.

"I see. Exactly, what does that make you?"

"The poor cottager's son."

"Of course." There was no missing the sardonic tone in Tristan's voice. "I'll wake Alain. It's going to be a long night, and it's no fun watching the sun rise alone."

Chapter Three

Giles paced the length of the elegant cherry-paneled study, his agitation evident in the furrow he'd worn in the thick-piled Axminster carpet, walking between the heavy cherry wood desk and the gracious bank of floor-to-ceiling windows that looked out over the south lawn. Leaning on the desk top, he planted his hands and pressed his weight against them, drawing deep breaths in the hopes of gathering his shaken composure.

Somewhere in his rational brain, he knew there was no real need to worry. She was a gypsy. What could she know of him and his family? Of his parents? Most likely, her claims were nothing more than a stab in the dark. She probably pulled this scam the length of the country. Still, he silently cursed the dysfunctional nature of his parents' marriage, his mother's mental instability, and his father's inability to recognize affection

41

when it was offered to him. All of which combined to create enough doubt that he had to take the lovely gypsy's claims with a certain degree of seriousness.

It was some consolation to know that despite her claims to the contrary, he would be able to foist her off with a large sum of money and in a week this farce would be over. But in the meantime, he felt as if he was on the brink of being physically ill. He'd been Trojan horsed.

Irina had come to Spelthorne, all earthy beauty and lovely seduction. The peaceful image she'd made sitting at his bedroom window was still freshly etched in his mind's eye. That moment existed in a suspended reality, an alternate reality, one in which she did not open her mouth and ruin the illusion. But she had and it became clear to Giles that she had come to his home deliberately to lay her claims.

It didn't matter that her claims would come to naught. He was still angry—something he seldom was. There was little cause to be angry or even to be upset in his well-ordered world, but Giles recognized the foreign emotion immediately. Warrior lords of old must have felt this way upon seeing an attacking army advancing on their holds, their homes. The comparison was apt. The gypsy's ploy was akin to a declaration of war. She'd put Spelthorne under siege.

He heard the door open but didn't turn around. He gathered another deep breath before he had to face Alain and Tristan. He was glad for Tristan's suggestion that they weather the night together, but it was deuced awkward to try and explain the situation. Glasses clinked on the side board.

"Brandy or whiskey, Giles?" Alain asked.

"Neither. I don't want to risk a muddled head," Giles said, turning to face Tristan and Alain.

Alain put down the glass he'd been preparing. "Good idea. I'll ring for coffee. We'll need that much at least to get through the night."

Giles nodded and motioned to the two men to take the chairs set in front of the desk. He took up his place behind the desk, needing the security it offered. The three of them might be more comfortable in the over-stuffed chairs set before the marble fireplace, but Giles needed the authority that went with sitting in the worn chair behind the desk from which he conducted so much of Spelthorne's business.

Tristan and Alain came and settled themselves. "Tristan told me the basics on the way down. What exactly does she base her claim on?" Alain began.

Giles spread the documents before them on the desk.

"A birth certificate and a diary?" Alain's skepticism was obvious.

"A birth certificate can be easily forged. Public records contain dates, and the parish records in the village would have the details she claims." Tristan dismissed the certificate as inconsequential.

"The diary could be complete fabrication. There's no way to know if its fiction or truth. Who would be able to validate its contents?" Alain suggested.

"Those are the arguments I made with her this

evening," Giles said, gratified that his friends shared his train of thought.

"Even if she believed the claims were legitimate, what can she do to push them?" Alain asked, lazily studying the onyx inkwell on the desk's corner. "Has she a fortune to spend on legal fees? Does she have a barrister who will take on her case? Is there anyone who will believe her?"

"Not that I know of." Giles grimaced and blew out a long breath. "Her very inability to pursue this is what bothers me most. From all aspects, it seems her cause is futile. It is dangerous to play the imposter, and yet she does. What does she hope to gain?" He pushed a hand through his disheveled hair.

"Money?" Tristan offered.

"I already offered her a tidy sum to take her game somewhere else. She turned it down. She wanted only the right to stay at Spelthorne until I read the diary."

"Did you grant the request?" Alain queried.

"Yes. I thought it would be best to keep her where I could see her until this was settled."

Tristan leaned forward, elbows on knees, chin on hands. "Then I think there is only one thing to do and that is read the diary. We can't decide a course of action until we know what is in there."

A footman scratched the door and entered with the heavy silver coffee service. He settled it on the low table by the fireplace, giving the three men a chance to rise and resettle themselves in the comfortable chairs. Alain poured steaming cups of coffee while Giles began to read out loud.

February 24, 1787

I am convinced I have conceived at last. I have called upon my husband, the earl's physician to verify my condition. Perhaps the birth of a child, of a son, will win me some affection and warmth from Spelthorne. I have long been of the belief that our marital estrangement has been due to the lack of children. It has been five years since our marriage—a long time to wait.

March 13, 1787

I am indeed expecting a child, and I am reminded of that every morning. I have been dreadfully ill, and I have lost weight in the early stages of this pregnancy. My clothes hang on my frame, and Spelthorne seems repulsed by my haggard appearance. To my regret, he greeted the news of our impending parenthood with neutral good form, saying all the correct things but none of the things I wished to hear. Since the announcement, he has taken himself back to London and no doubt the mistress he keeps there. He has indicated he will return in time for his heir's birth in September, and I am free to send for him before then if there is need. I am not welcome in London this season and I find myself alone in the country with few people for company this time of year.

"Their life doesn't sound all that different than other couples I know," Tristan said while Giles leafed ahead in the diary. "Nor does it sound all that original. This could be any noblewoman's diary. Perhaps she found it at a flea market and made a few alterations."

Alain perked up from his habitual slouch. "Giles, do you have any of your mother's correspondence left? Letters she wrote? We can match the handwriting."

"There may be some left in the safe. I have a box of her things in there." Giles stood up and passed the diary to Tristan. "It's your turn to read while I open the safe. Skip ahead to the parts closer to the birth. The earlier months look like more of the same, complaints over pregnancy and loneliness. No matter how cursory the entries are, the theme is clear. She was eager for my father's approval, and she was denied it." Hurt was evident in his voice, and he wished he'd had control enough to hide it. He didn't want his friends to see him so vulnerable. His father had been a hard man, taciturn and stoic in his ways, despite his handsome looks. Giles knew himself to have his share of good looks, but up until tonight he'd always been thankful that people thought he took after his mother with his golden hair and blue eyes. Now, he wished he might have looked a bit more like his father, darker with hazel eyes. It would have gone some distance in alleviating the seeds of doubt in his mind.

Tristan took the book hesitantly. "Are you sure? This is private, perhaps it would be better if you read it."

Giles shook his head. "No. If there's any truth to Irina's claims, it's best you know everything from the start." He strode behind the desk and knelt down to begin fiddling with the safe. Tristan's voice came low and firm from the fireplace.

August 12, 1787
The baby is a boy, I know it. It kicks lustily and often, which is an uncomfortable consolation for all I have had to endure alone. The heat of the summer has been miserable. My ankles have swollen to three times their size, and I've become a lumbering ox. I alternately wish for Spelthorne's presence and am thankful for his absence. I am not the least bit desirable in my current state. I am already planning my wardrobe for the season next year. It will be delightful to wear fashionable clothing again and to dance in dainty slippers.

August 20, 1787
To alleviate the boredom of my life in the country, I have let the gypsy's camp on the corner of Spelthorne Abbey. I took my maid and walked to their camp today for something to do. I saw the fortune-teller, a handsome, determined sort of woman named Magda, who I judged to be in her late twenties. She also acts as a healer for the caravan, and has an interesting knowledge of herbs. Her knowledge of herbs was far better than her fortune-telling ability, for she predicted that my child would be a daughter.

August 21, 1787

I received devastating news from Spelthorne today. Parliament has closed, and he is off to a friend's country house. He tells me to send word of his child's birth to this address. If it is a male heir he will return home to celebrate. If not, he will return home after grouse hunting, and we can try again. I am devastated and angry. I had so hoped a child would be the answer to our flagging marriage, but now I despair of anything short of a son repairing a marriage that was broken from the start. I see now that he desired a traditional society marriage, despite the intensity of his courtship so many years ago.

I cannot shake the gypsy's fortune, and I doubt my earlier belief that a child will be a son although no other option can be considered. I will not doom a daughter of mine to the empty existence that has become my life as a countess. Spelthorne would shun a daughter. She would be ignored as I am.

August 30, 1787

Doctor Tallbridge assures me there is not much longer to wait for the arrival of the child. Indeed, I spent most of the day lying down and suffering pains although the doctor noted there was no progress towards being delivered. There was, however, blood, and I thought Doctor Tallbridge was more concerned than he let on.

September 16, 1787
I have taken a turn for the worse. I cannot get out of bed, and the bleeding continues. Doctor Tallbridge can do nothing until true labor begins. I called earlier today for the gypsy, Magda, in the hopes that she has knowledge of an herb that can safely stimulate the birth of the child. She came and listened to my belly and put her hands on it. She said the baby must be born soon. The child is in distress. She has herbs to give me although they carry some risk of their own. But I am desperate to birth this child and be done with pregnancy.

"Did you find those letters yet, Giles?" Tristan called, setting down the book.

"Not yet. Keep reading." Giles said in muffled tones from behind the desk.

"It's Alain's turn. I have to say all this feminine writing about birthing makes me uneasy. I feel quite intrusive reading about it," Tristan complained.

Alain gave a bark of laughter. "I didn't think you were squeamish about anything, Tristan. Alright, where did we leave off? Oh yes, the herbs."

There was an extended silence. Giles stood up. "Alain, you're supposed to read out loud."

Alain's voice was soft and shocked when he spoke. "I know. There's nothing written again until September 24th." Alain gulped hard. "I don't know if I can read this out loud." He held the book out to Giles, his eyes filled with a kind of horror. "Please, take it."

Giles went to him and gingerly took the battered red book. He settled into his chair, not missing the worried glances that passed between Tristan and Alain. He steeled himself as best he could. After all, he knew what was most likely written in the next entry. Irina had told him as much earlier. He knew what had to be there if Irina had any support for her outrageous claim. Despite his efforts to neutralize his reaction, Giles scanned the first few lines and knew he could not read the entry out loud either.

He read deliberately, taking in each word and imprinting it in his mind in the hopes that reading this story would not be necessary again. Afterward, he closed his eyes and pinched the bridge of his nose, seeking some sort of clarity but none came. The terrible litany of *it's true, it's true. Everything Irina said was true* ran mercilessly through his head. Oh God, what was he going to do?

"It's all true," Giles said at last, breaking the uncomfortable silence that blanketed the room. "Everything she said is right there in the diary." It was a terrible truth too—the lengths to which one woman had gone to win the affections of a husband incapable of giving them. The story served as a strong moral in regards to allowing oneself to be swept away on the tides of passion. "It's all there. There was a daughter sent to the gypsies and replaced by a cottager's illegitimate son."

"Of course the diary collaborates her story," Tristan interjected swiftly. "She would not have shown it to you otherwise. That doesn't prove the diary is authentic. For all we know, she made the story up and hired someone to write it down. Truly, Giles, the story proves less than you think. It would have made no sense for her to show you a diary that didn't collaborate her tale."

Giles nodded, grateful for the devious twists and turns of Tristan's mind. Tristan's thoughts did ease the knot of fear residing in his chest. "It is difficult to believe someone would go to such lengths to undermine another's life," Giles said.

"Believe it. When there's money involved, people will do almost anything," Tristan said grimly. "After seven years of espionage work for the crown, I believe people are capable of anything, no matter how inhumane or how improbable."

"There is still the consideration of the letters," Alain spoke up. "Did you find any handwriting samples?"

"Yes, they're on the desk." Giles rose to get the pile he left behind when Alain had asked him to read the fateful diary entry. "I rather wish I hadn't found them." He passed the packet to Alain who slipped the first one out of its envelope and opened it.

Alain laid the letter next to a randomly selected diary entry and grimaced. "I had hoped the handwriting would be vastly different."

Giles picked the letter up and scanned the contents. "The writing style is the same as well, very succinct, very direct and to the point. My mother was not one to waste words."

"More to the point," Tristan drawled, long legs spread out in front of him. "Was she actually capable of what Irina claims?"

Giles met Alain's eyes, a wealth of childhood memories passing in that single glance. Tristan had not met them until they had gone to Eton but Giles and Alain had grown up together on neighboring summer estates in the Lake District. The threesome might have known each other for over fifteen years, but Alain and Giles had known each other over twenty.

"I forget, Tristan, that you did not know my parents. In the years I knew my mother, I would have to say yes. Her entire focus was my father. She alternated from being desperate for his favor and being furious at him for withholding it. She craved his affection. I have long thought it was his behavior toward her that drove her insane in the end." Another reason why love was so bloody dangerous. Unrequited love had no recourse.

Giles tinkered with the lid of an expensive, inlaid trifle box that sat on a table next to his chair. "She had a boating accident on the lake the summer before we met at school." He neglected to say she'd gone out on the lake during a late summer storm and had no business trying to man the oars herself. But she'd been angry with his father yet again over some imagined or real slight. It had been hard to tell the difference in those last days when her sanity had been in question.

Giles passed a hand over his mouth as if he feared what might come out of it if he kept talking. "I think I'd like to be alone." He said quietly.

"No." Tristan said firmly, surprising Giles with the force of his refusal. Tristan rose and began to pace. "If we leave you alone, you will sit here and be maudlin. You're giving up far too easily, and that is exactly what this woman hopes for. At best, she has found a chink in your family armor—the estrangement between your mother and father—and she has extrapolated it into a fantastical fairy tale. You're not even trying to fight."

"Tristan, you don't understand. We have to be very careful to avoid a scandal. This must be handled delicately," Giles protested.

"Oh yes, we'll be discreet," Tristan said, stopping at the window to stroke his chin and study the lightening landscape. "We'll call her down here as soon as it's light. We'll tell her she can take us to court—which of course she can't afford to do, and even if she could the system is so backlogged it will take years to get a hearing. If we stick to our position, she'll have to back down. She hasn't the wherewithal to see us in court. Then, Giles, you'll write her a nice check and send her on her way."

"She won't take money. Remember, I already tried that?"

"She didn't take it because she thought she had a bigger fish to land. Once she realizes she cannot possibly win, she'll be happy enough to take your check."

"What if she's telling the truth?" Giles asked. "I can't send her away knowing that I've wronged her. My God, do you realize the enormity of the truth? Of what she's been denied?"

Tristan rounded on Giles, anger evident in the depths

of his brown eyes. "I do realize the enormity of this! I am trying to find a way to protect Spelthorne and all you've worked for from a fortune hunter. What does she know about running an estate? She will ruin your entire life's ambition within three years, if not sooner. You can't doom your tenants to that. They adore you."

Tristan lowered his voice, some of his frustration gone. "I am trying to protect you as well. You are Spelthorne. You've worked your whole life to be the earl, and I am not going to step aside and let your damnable honor get the best of you, not when you're the best earl I've ever met. I've yet to meet someone who cares for his land with the devotion you show."

"Thank you," Giles said quietly, overwhelmed by the sentiments Tristan voiced. Tristan had never spoken to him in such a manner before, and to know that one's friends cared so deeply for him nearly undid him.

"We don't have to acknowledge her claim. We can squelch it right now and have her gone by breakfast." Tristan said again, his gaze returning to the window.

"I cannot live a life made out of a wrong done to another. There is enough truth in the diary, the handwriting, the birth certificate, to need further clarification. If nothing else, further clarification will strengthen our case and weaken hers." Giles stood his ground firmly.

"And if further probing reveals her claim to have merit?" Tristan asked.

"Then we'll make those decisions at that time. I hope it will not come to that," Giles said calmly. Now that the initial shock was over, he could begin planning the next step and that made him feel immeasurably better.

He saw the tic in Tristan's cheek jump in silent disapproval, but to his credit Tristan said nothing, merely stared out the window with his arms crossed, his gaze hard.

"What shall we do now?" Alain asked.

"We shall send for the vicar. He is up north outside of York. It will take a while for him to be found and to make the trip. In the meanwhile, Irina will be our guest. We'll pass her off as a distant relation. We'll take her to the horse fair with us so I can keep an eye on her until the house party is over. I don't want her running loose in the house and raising eyebrows. It would be best to introduce her quietly and upfront so no one thinks we're hiding anything."

Alain nodded his support. "With that settled, I shall catch a bit of sleep and see you in the main hall at ten for the fair. Cecile is looking forward to the outing." He pressed a hand on Giles's shoulder in support as he walked past him to the door. "We'll get through this, you know, all of us together just like we've gotten through everything else."

Giles smiled for the first time since finding Irina in his bedroom. "I know. Thank you." It hadn't been that long ago they'd rallied to Alain's support when he thought he'd lost Cecile in the political turmoil of post-Napoleon France. Nor had it been more than a handful years when they'd held baited breaths around Tristan's sickbed after he'd been shot by a rogue agent. The wound had nearly proved fatal.

Alain cocked his head in Tristan's direction. "He'll come around. He's just more protective of our circle than we realize."

The door shut behind Alain, leaving Tristan with Giles. "I'm sorry Chatham isn't here," Tristan said suddenly, referring to the long-absent fourth member of their circle.

Giles tidied up the desk, shuffling papers he'd taken out of the safe. Chatham's desertion was still a great mystery even to him who was perhaps closest to Chatham. "I wouldn't be surprised if he was in America. He'd been talking about that when we were all together for Alain-Alexander's christening. But that seems ages ago," he said with a lightness he didn't feel.

Tristan said nothing, only nodded. "I would offer to send for him but I don't know where to look. If I thought anyone at Whitehall knew where he was . . ." Tristan broke off and shrugged his shoulders.

"It's alright. The three of us are enough. It's probably just as you said, nothing more than a poor attempt to exploit a weak link in the family." Giles forced a smile. "I am off to freshen up so my guests don't suspect I spent the night poorly." He paused a moment, debating how to say what he had to. "Tristan, I would like to ask you not to tell Isabella. Not yet."

Tristan looked dubious. "She's bound to ask what we were doing all night. I can hardly tell her we were playing cards. You know she will be discreet. Is there a reason to hide any of this from her? She's stood your friend for years just as the rest of us have."

"Alain hasn't seen the gypsy. But you did," Giles began.

Tristan nodded, not following Giles's direction. "Just briefly and in the dark at that."

"I know, but I think you would recognize her in the light of day. Her name is Irina Dupeski," Giles said bluntly, knowing that his friend had an uncommon talent for remembering everything from the most trivial detail on up.

Tristan's face clouded momentarily. "The fortune-teller that night at Denbigh's party when I had first returned from the continent. Bella never did like her." Tristan couldn't suppress a short laugh. "Do you remember how mad Bella was that her fortune was all bad while the rest of ours was quite glamorous?"

Giles gave a small smile. "I remember. Irina will go by the name Cate while she's here. Perhaps once she's dressed up and with a different name, Isabella won't recall her."

"Well, we can try although I don't like keeping secrets from my wife." Tristan grimaced. "I'll have Isabella send over some extra gowns for her, but if she finds out who's been wearing her clothes, you will pay for it, not me." Tristan wagged a warning finger at Giles.

"Mea culpa," Giles agreed. "We'll put out the tale that she's a shirttail relative and is late arriving because of a carriage accident or some such incident." Giles sobered from the brief moment of levity that had seized them.

"I do mean to fight, Tristan. No one will take Spelthorne from me but I can't simply turn her away without knowing the truth."

Tristan met his gaze. "Darn right no one will take Spelthorne."

"Thank you. I'll see you in a few hours." Giles inclined his head graciously and departed.

Chapter Four

Irina stretched, stiff from her nightlong vigil at the window seat. She had been too restless to take advantage of the luxurious bed in her chamber. In any case, she had been too guilt-ridden to sleep. The pain on Giles's face had cut her. She felt the lowest of trollops for what she had done and how she had done it.

The truth should be easier than this. For a moment he had wanted her, seen something wonderful in her, then that dark friend of his barged in and ruined it, probably for the best. Nothing good could come from indulging with Giles Moncrief. An interlude with him would only cloud the issues between them.

From her window seat she could see the library with its elegant curve of windows. It had not filled her with a sense of victory to know that Giles had spent the night in there, most likely poring over the diary and conferring with his trusted friends. They had probably spent the night planning their strategies, ways to discredit her, ways to win in and out of the court system.

A man like Giles would leave no stone unturned, no pathway unexplored when it came to protecting what he felt was his. She had expected nothing less. She should have felt heartened that she'd won this first round; her request to stay at the abbey until all was settled had been granted, and she'd gotten him to look at the diary. She would gladly claim the victory although the truth was that she wasn't sure how it would have turned out if Viscount Gresham hadn't barged in and accidentally forced Giles's hand.

Magda had practically danced about the room when Irina had rung for her in the kitchens and reported all that had transpired. In the midst of the behind the scenes hubbub of serving dinner, it had been relatively easy for Magda to insinuate herself among the maids and valets in the servants' quarters to wait for Irina's summons. Irina had summoned Magda immediately after being escorted to her chambers. Now Magda snored gently on a soft pallet in the large dressing room off the bedchamber, undisturbed by the doubts and worries that had kept Irina awake all night.

A knock sounded at the door, and Irina rose to answer it, hastily patting her hair. Surely Giles hadn't finished the diary already, but who else could it be? No one else knew she was here.

A maid stood in the hall, several dresses carefully laid over her arms. "Miss Cate, the earl thought you would find these dresses useful since your trunks were damaged in the carriage accident. A dreadful happening to be sure, but you're here now, safe and unhurt at last." Any surprise the maid may have had over the door being answered by the lady herself and not her maid was quickly disguised in a flow of chatter and a bustle of activity as she swept past Irina and started fussing over the dresses.

Irina desperately tried to follow the one-sided conversation, knowing it was vital to understanding what Giles expected of her, how he was explaining her presence to the staff.

"Ah yes, my maid and I were lucky to escape injury," Irina confirmed, looking at the dresses laid out on the bed. They were exquisite and far finer than the few gowns she'd had made for the occasion. Not for the first time, she was swamped with a sense of inadequacy. What did she know about being a lady? She'd thought the gowns she'd purchased were quite fine. The price had certainly indicated as much. But the gowns spread before her were far more expensive and of much better quality.

Her first thought was that Giles had been quite kind to think of her and what she might wear. Her second thought was where the gowns had come from. She hoped they didn't belong to the elegant lady who'd been on Giles's arm most of the evening. It would be the cruelest of intentions to have her wear the gowns of his mistress. It would be the ultimate put down, the ultimate reminder of her place. It was hard to imagine

Giles would resort to such an underhanded tactic. Then again, he had no reason to treat her well after what she'd disclosed last evening.

"It was kind of the earl to think of me. Where did he find clothes on such short notice?" She asked, probing for information and hoping her question wasn't as transparent as it sounded.

"They're Lady Isabella's, the viscount's wife," the maid said reverently, in apparent awe. "I know it is early, but we'll need time to alter the gowns." The maid gave her an assessing gaze. "The viscount's wife is taller, so we'll need to shorten everything four or five inches. We'll have to hurry. The earl and his guests are leaving for the horse fair at ten o'clock sharp."

That brought Irina up short. He meant for her to go with the house party? She had thought to keep to her quarters. Admittedly, the thought of going to the horse fair was more appealing than staying cooped up in her rooms all day. But it also filled her with trepidation. What could he mean by including her? There was no time to consider what game he might be playing. The maid gestured toward the gowns.

"Which do you prefer, miss?"

She must play the lady, Irina told herself. She clearly recognized that two of the dresses were for dancing or dinner. They were far too exquisite for a carriage ride and a fair. But the remaining three were all day dresses, and she could not discern their specific functions. It would not help her cause to appear in less than appropriate garb.

Irina gave a regal wave of her hand. "Choose one for me. I will wake my maid to help you."

Three hours later, Irina twisted and turned in the dressing room's long pier glass to see the back of her dress. "It's lovely!" she exclaimed to Magda.

The maid had selected the cherry-striped muslin with its square neckline trimmed in tiny white lace. Three-quarter length sleeves were gathered slightly above her elbow and dripped with falls of yet more lace.

Irina lifted the hem of the dress to peep at the leather half boots beneath. The borrowed shoes were only slightly too wide and the alterations had been minimal. In spite of the need for hemming, the gown had fit well enough although it had been a bit loose in the waist. The maid had skillfully fixed that with a satin sash.

A wide-brimmed straw bonnet trimmed in grosgrain ribbon to match the gown along with a pair of ladies gloves and a delicate white parasol lay on a footstool ready to complete the ensemble. The viscount's wife had thought of everything from the luxurious silk stockings to the filmy wrap she could secure about her shoulders.

"I look like a real lady." Irina gave a final twirl. Satisfied, she crossed to her small trunk and began rummaging.

"Enough with that 'real lady' talk," Magda snapped from her perch on the arm of a chair. "You are a real lady, manor born. Stop acting as if this is something you're pretending to be. This is who you are."

Irina straightened, a black pouch in her hand. "You are sure I am not pretending, aren't you? You are certain that I am Catherine Moncrief?" Her doubts were obvious. What if the story had become garbled over the years, if Magda had gotten confused? If Magda was using her for some nefarious purpose, one last scam? Who could blame her for wanting comfort and convenience in her later years? But Irina didn't want to be an unwitting tool in that kind of scheme.

Magda scowled, the lines on her careworn face deepening. "The earl doesn't doubt it. He's keeping you in sight. He's invited you along today to keep an eye on you. He doesn't want you running about where you can cause trouble."

Irina smiled weakly and nodded. So much for the fairy tale. Of course Magda was right. Giles couldn't abandon his guests, and he could not leave her alone in the house. It had been nice to imagine for awhile that Giles had desired her company.

Irina opened the pouch and spilled a delicate necklace into her palm. "Should I wear it?"

Magda shook her head. "No. It's too soon. Save it as a last trump."

Irina replaced it and pulled the strings of the bag, tucking it away in her trunk. "It's time to go. I can hear foot traffic in the hall. Everyone must be moving downstairs."

Magda softened. "Remember who you are, and you'll do fine. You've plenty of spunk in you. Just be yourself." Magda patted her hand.

"That's good because I don't how to be anyone else,"

Irina retorted. She would get through the awkwardness of today with her head up and her pride intact just as she'd gotten through countless other difficult situations in her life. If she could handle the rowdiness of a tavern, she could certainly manage a genteel outing to a horse fair.

With her parasol furled in one gloved hand and her reticule in the other, Irina sailed out the door of the room to join the rest of the party in the entry foyer. She paused at the top of the stairs, gripping the carved banister. Women dressed in colorful muslin gowns much like hers milled among men dressed in riding clothes, chattering gaily to one another. She drew a deep breath. The moment she stepped on those stairs, she would be Miss Cate, no longer Caterina Dupeski.

She spotted Giles immediately, picking out his golden hair and broad shoulders. He looked relaxed as he moved among his guests, stopping here and there to make brief inquiries. He paused at the group containing the woman Irina had seen with him the prior evening and bowed extravagantly over her hand, kissing it. Then he looked up and saw her and something sparked in his eyes. The woman saw it too and followed his gaze up the steps to where she stood.

There was no choice now. She had to move down the staircase to where Giles was waiting. He was turned out impeccably in buff breeches, riding boots, and a dark blue coat suitable for the outing. His white linen was crisp and spotless, a characteristic Irina was coming to quickly associate with him. His personal appearance was always immaculate, and he took great pride in being well turned out in all aspects of his appearance and hygiene. He smelled of soap and spices when she placed her hand on the arm he offered her. She knew he'd spent a restless night but all signs of sleeplessness and worry were carefully concealed.

"Good morning, Cate. I trust you found the items the maid brought to your room satisfactory?" He inquired graciously. It was hard to remember it was all just an act when he stood next to her paying her such polite attention.

"Yes, thank you. It was kind of you to see to my welfare after the carriage accident," she said, indicating she'd fully understood the maid's chatter.

Giles's other hand closed over the top of hers briefly where it rested on his sleeve. "Very good. We are in accord then. Let me introduce you to a few of our guests."

He drew her through the crowd of guests to his group of close friends and presented her to Alain, Tristan, and their wives. It was awkward. Alain and Tristan greeted her politely but with reserve. Of course, they knew why she was here and were determined to protect Giles. To them, she was the enemy. She hadn't expected them to greet her with any enthusiasm.

Cecile and Isabella did not know. They were warm and friendly. Isabella discreetly assured her in low undertones that she looked fabulous in the cherry muslin and that she had not worn it yet. Her disguise must be effective. Isabella showed no sign of recognizing her from the Denbigh's party years ago.

"Cate, you'll be in good hands here. I must go and

organize the carriages," Giles said, catching her by surprise. The name was unfamiliar to her. She had been Irina or Caterina all her life. She had known laying claim to Spelthorne would change her life in multiple ways but it was something of a blow to realize how completely her life would change right down to her name. If she won her claim, she would no longer be, could no longer be, Caterina Dupeski. Suddenly, Cate seemed to fit, a cross between Caterina and Catherine—who she was and who she'd always been.

She paid half-hearted attention to the small talk flowing about her, finding that she was having a rather difficult time tearing her gaze away from following Giles as he went about his duties. Isabella and Cecile made polite inquiries, and she answered as best she could. After a bit, Cecile gave up and nodded to where Giles stood just outside the hall on the front verandah directing people to carriages. "He's very good at sorting out people."

Cate felt herself blush. "Yes, he is." There was no sense denying it. She'd been squarely caught in the act.

The hall had emptied out efficiently, leaving only their little cluster. Giles gestured to them and they trooped out to the verandah.

"I've put the four of you in the landau. I'll take Cate up in the curricle with me," Giles directed.

Tristan gave Giles a questioning look. "Are you sure you wouldn't be more comfortable with Alain and Cecile? Bella and I have wanted to try out those bays of yours." He nodded to where a tiger held the heads of the spirited team harnessed to the yellow curricle.

"I've wanted to put them through their paces, myself. They haven't been worked properly for too long," Giles said smoothly. Tristan nodded his assent, and everyone climbed aboard their respective vehicles.

Giles handed her up onto the seat, and Cate nervously fiddled with her skirts. She felt his weight on the seat as he settled beside her and took up the reins, clucking to the horses.

Cate kept her eyes forward, trying not to give into the temptation of staring at the handsome man on the seat next to her, so close that their thighs touched as the curricle jounced down the road on its two wheels.

"Your friends think you need protection," she commented, referring to Tristan's offer to take the curricle so that she and Giles would not be alone.

Giles laughed at that, a merry, loud sound that appeared to be genuine as he threw back his head and let the breeze ruffle his hair. "Tristan's been itching to get his hands on these bays since June. If I'd let him drive, he would have raced this gig all the way to Staines. We're all horse mad, you know."

He gave her a jolly wink that provoked a sense of longing deep inside her—a longing for this day with its beautiful weather and the handsome man beside her to be real, not merely the forced product of her actions.

"Besides, you and I need to talk. This might be the only privacy we have all day." His words reminded her vividly of how contrived this glorious moment was. She was with him only because circumstances dictated that she was too dangerous for him to be left alone.

Cate straightened on the narrow seat and tried to put a bit of meager distance between their jouncing thighs. She kept her tone brisk. "Telling the maid the story of my 'circumstances' was clever. Be assured, I listened avidly to her chatter this morning." He needed to be reminded that she was no green girl of seventeen, fresh from the isolation of the schoolroom. She was a woman full-grown who had seen much of life and knew her own mind. Any weakness she showed him was sure to be exploited.

"There is more to it than a mishap with your vehicle. People will want to know who you are. You are Lady Cate Winthrop."

"Winthrop was mother's name before she married," Cate said quietly, almost reverently. "Are you sure that would be appropriate?"

"Absolutely," Giles remarked stiffly, clearly not caring to be second guessed. "Simply, you are to be called Lady Cate as is the custom when addressing the daughter of an earl, marquis, or duke. In this case, the daughter of an earl. On occasion, people may refer to you as Miss Cate."

"I know who my mother was," Cate cut in sharply. This was a dangerous moment. She could not sit there quietly and let him lecture her about the state of the family. If she truly was Celeste Moncrief's daughter, she would know about her own mother. "She was Celeste Winthrop, daughter of the Earl of Stonebridge, before she married father."

Giles gave a curt nod of his head and clucked to the horses, slapping the reins. His jaw clenched, and Cate knew she'd annoyed him with her acerbic reply. She drew a deep breath and tried to soften the moment. He might hate what she was here to do, but perhaps he didn't have to hate her.

"Who would you like me to be? Should Lady Cate be a cousin?"

"A very distant cousin," Giles said. "If anyone asks for specifics, you can make an airy gesture and say something about a far-flung branch of the family tree."

"Ah, a fourth cousin then?" She'd meant only to tease.

"No!" Giles snapped. "Do not dare to be so specific. We cannot risk anyone being interested enough to trace the family line."

"Oof!" The curricle hit a rut in the road, and Cate was tossed against Giles. She landed against the strength of his shoulder and grabbed at his arm to right herself.

"Are you alright?" Giles inquired with gentlemanly reserve.

Cate blew out a breath. "Only a bit jarred." In truth, she felt more shaken from the contact with the muscled hardness of his body than the jolt itself. The curricle lurched again, and she clutched at his arm once more to steady herself. "I'd much rather ride on a horse than a buggy any day," she said awkwardly, feeling self conscience and yet not able to trust her own balance against the jouncing road, in order to release her hold on his arm.

She was further embarrassed to see Giles cast a disparaging glance downward to where her hand gripped his sleeve.

"That's another thing we must address," Giles said

sternly. "What happened in my chambers last night cannot be repeated. As a gentleman, I need to apologize for allowing that kiss to happen."

She should accept his apology demurely and say nothing, but his prickly attitude and high-handed manner with which he'd conducted the entire conversation roused her temper and left her feeling querulous. "Well, I should think so. Being dropped unceremoniously on one's backside is hardly what one expects when one is being so thoroughly seduced by a peer of the realm." She was tempted to add that she hadn't been entirely surprised since he was really a peer, but she heeded the warning in the set of his jaw and held the retort. She had tweaked him far enough.

"Seduced!" Giles fired a sidelong glance of disbelief at her. "*You* started it."

"I most certainly did not!" She snapped, feeling color flood her cheeks. Had she? Come to think of it, she couldn't remember how it had started, only that it had felt wonderful until the viscount had barged in and taken them by surprise. Her bottom and ankle were both still slightly tender from the fall.

Giles was insistent. "Regardless, we must have a pact that such a thing cannot happen again."

"Didn't you like it? I thought you did." Cate pouted innocently and stared out across the landscape, deliberately avoiding his gaze. The traffic was picking up now and the pennants flying from the top of canopies in the distance signaled they were nearing Staines. The bittersweet novelty of riding with Giles and looking the part of a fashionable lady, all the while sparring with the man beside her, was coming to a close.

Giles must have sensed the end was near as well. Desperation tinged the edges of his voice. "Look, we have a deuced awkward situation between us. It seems that for both our sakes we must attempt to be allies until the situation can be resolved. To speak plainly, I cannot leave you to your own devices, so we must be seen socially and appear to be on good terms, as one would expect of relatives."

Cate looked about her at the nearby carriages on the road and noticed other women had their parasols up. Casually, she reached for her parasol and flicked it up. With a wide-eyed stare that would have done the most vacuous of debutantes proud, Cate said, "I'm sorry, I thought you said something about 'for both of our sakes.' I've yet to hear what I get out of this. It sounds like my good behavior is important only as far your benefits."

"As long as you behave, you get to stay." Giles bit out as he steered the curricle under the shade of a tree near the fairgrounds. Others from the house party were parking their conveyances nearby and dismounting.

"Hah! That's as toothless as threats come, Giles Moncrief. You wouldn't dare to throw me out." Cate laughed.

"Try me."

Cate laughed again, knowing she hadn't dared to go any farther. She was smart enough to know when the game was over, at least for now. "Alright, truce. We'll behave as you suggest. I agree, it is the clearest way to seeing our needs met."

"Thank you." Giles tossed his reins to the waiting tiger and leapt down. "Wait there, I'll help you out."

He came around to her side, and Cate furled her parasol. She smiled down at him with what she hoped was cousinly affection, although she privately thrilled to the feel of his strong hands about her waist as he lifted her down. He settled her on the ground and she was aware he kept his hands on her waist a bit longer than necessary, under the guise of allowing her a chance to adjust her skirts.

She smiled at him, sensing that a certain level of levity had returned to their banter. Her lips lifted in a teasing lilt, but the laughing words she'd thought to toss back at him died on her lips. Over Giles's shoulder Lady Fox-Haughton was approaching, and Cate knew enough about women of any station to know she wasn't pleased at finding her man in the arms of another.

Chapter Five

If the situation with his newly minted 'cousin Cate' was deuced awkward, the ensuing scene with Lady Fox-Haughton promised to be something else entirely. In this case, deuced awkward didn't even begin to cover it. Giles stepped back from Cate and released his grip on her slender waist. For a man who prided himself on avoiding such unpleasant entanglements, he'd done a poor job of it over the last eighteen hours.

Candice Wetherby, the Lady Fox-Haughton, swept forward regally and planted herself on Giles's right side with a proprietary air.

"Spelthorne, there you are. I knew you'd be bringing up the back, dedicated as you are to seeing to your guests' comforts first." As always, she was attired impeccably from the excellent cut of her apple-green muslin walking dress to the tips of her extravagant leather half boots, dyed to match the gown.

Usually Giles admired her modish appearance, but the sight of her stylish perfection did not stir the requisite appreciation within him. Today she looked like a beautifully dressed shell against the backdrop of the agitated yet animated conversation he'd held with Cate on the drive.

Of course the idea that she was a shell wasn't true. She was a leading political hostess and intelligent in her own right. It was those qualities along with her sense of style that had originally brought her to his attention. Lady Fox-Haughton was not a vacuous shell of a woman, and he'd do well to remember it.

"Lady Cate is it?" The glint in her sharp hazel eyes warned she was sharpening her claws and her tongue. All her attention was riveted on his dubious guest. "We did not get to converse in the hall before departing. Tell me how you've come to know Spelthorne."

It took all of Giles's self control not to leap into the conversation and answer on Cate's behalf. But he realized to do so would put Candice on the scent more surely than anything else he could devise.

Cate did not disappoint. She looked Lady Fox-Haughton in the eye and smiled conversationally. "I am Lady Cate Winthrop. My carriage broke down so I did not arrive until very late last evening."

Giles watched Candice take in the information and process it behind shrewd, knowing eyes. "How terrible for you, my dear," Candice sympathized, but Giles wasn't fooled for a moment. "Winthrop you say? That would be Spelthorne's mother's name."

He had wanted to avoid this. Candice had practically memorized DeBrett's peerage right down to the most minor of baronets. He did not doubt she'd paid special attention to the Spelthorne entry.

She tapped a long gloved finger against her chin thoughtfully. "So you must be a cousin of sorts?"

"Yes," Cate offered.

"Yes? Is that all?" Candice pressed much to Giles's dislike. "There are all sorts of cousins—first cousins, second cousins, kissing cousins." She laughed at her little joke, but Giles heard the ice beneath it.

What did she know? He regretted putting her room so close to his own chambers. She was three doors down from him. It was not entirely out of the realm of possibility that she'd heard or seen Cate walk down the hall last night. However, that assumption could also be putting the cart before the proverbial horse. She might not have seen anything more than him helping Cate down from the curricle and his indiscretion there, slight as it was.

He was saved from answering by the timely intervention of Alain and Cecile, who fairly swooped down on them, irrevocably disrupting the conversation.

"Giles, I want to find Cecile a nice, docile mare. You must come and tell me who the best horse sellers are," Alain said congenially with a wide grin that implied he knew exactly what he had done.

"Spelthorne, go on with your friend," Candice waved her hand magnanimously. "It will give me a chance to get to know your cousin better."

Giles blanched. He had not expected this turn of events. Cecile saved him with a Gallic pout. "Oh, I was so hoping Lady Cate would help me select some lace from the vendors." She turned exclusively to Cate. "I've been admiring the lace fall on your sleeves, and I thought you could offer suggestions."

"I would be delighted." Cate crooked her arm through Cecile's and began chattering at once, pausing after she'd walked a few yards to look over her shoulder as an afterthought and say, "Perhaps another time, Lady Fox-Haughton?"

Giles breathed easier knowing Cate was safely ensconced within Isabella and Cecile's protection. They wouldn't let Candice within fifty yards of her. Despising Candice as they did, the two of them enjoyed thwarting her efforts on any level. It would be a great relief to know Cate was with them as long as Tristan hadn't tipped off her identity to Isabella.

"What do you see in her?" Alain asked as they moved off to view the horse stalls.

"She has a somewhat substantiated claim to Spelthorne Abbey," Giles said. "I'd rather keep her close than let her alone to sow trouble." His eyes followed the women at the vending stalls in the distance.

"No. Not her. I meant Lady Fox-Haughton. None of us can stand her. Does she think you'll propose? She acts as if it's *fait accompli*."

"She and I have an understanding of convenience. After all, I'm not likely to find another hostess with her skills and entrée. It's a very practical arrangement. If she expects more, she'll be disappointed, but I doubt she does. She's a practical woman who understands the world."

Alain snorted. "There's no arguing that, Giles. She understands the world well enough to know how much she can accomplish for herself and how much she needs a man to do the rest. Lady Fox-Haughton is notoriously ambitious and knows exactly what an upstanding peer of your caliber can do for her political ambitions. She wants to be the wife of a prime minister."

Giles thrust his hands deep in his trouser pockets as they sauntered. "Then she'll be doubly disappointed in me. On no front will I be able to please her."

"Are you going to tell her about our Lady Cate?"

It was Giles's turn to snort in disbelief. "What do you think?"

"Right-o then," Alain said somewhat awkwardly. "I wouldn't tell her either."

Their arrival at the long length of rope stalls provided an end to their conversation. A sorrel mare of medium proportions whickered, drawing their attention. Alain went to it and lay a soothing hand on her long face, crooning soft words as he gave the horse a cursory once-over look.

"Just the sort of horse I was hoping to find for Cecile. She's game enough to learn to ride but I think we all terrify her with our big horses and hedge jumping."

Alain hunkered down to look at the horse's legs, running an expert hand over the fetlocks, testing for damaged tendons.

The mare looked promising, and they told the owner they'd be back after they'd looked over the rest of the stock.

It was half past one when they rejoined the group from the house party, congregating under the shady boughs of a spreading oak. Giles's servants had arrived with picnic supplies and erected a large white canopy and laid out a cold collation for his guests, complete with ice cold lemonade for the ladies and ale for the men. Everyone was in good spirits from the food and morning well spent among the excitement of a country fair.

He and Alain easily spotted Tristan and the ladies and went to join them. Cate was chatting effortlessly with Cecile and Isabella as Giles came up beside her.

"I see you found some lace." Giles nodded to the brown paper-wrapped package in Cecile's basket.

"Yes. I found the perfect trim." Cecile's sherry eyes danced with mischief. "I also found the perfect length of ribbon for Cate's hair but she refused to purchase it. I think you could persuade her, Giles. It would be the ideal souvenir for your cousin so she would remember her day at our little fair."

Giles reprimanded himself inwardly. Of all the things to forget! He'd not remembered she would need some walking around money. A lady of even modest station would have a few guineas in her reticule for such small purchases. Outwardly he smiled and gave a small bow to Cecile. "After luncheon I am yours to command. We shall go to the ribbon vendors and then on to look at the mares Alain thought would be suitable for you."

"Spelthorne, darling, I've heard the most delectable bit of news." Candice sailed up and inserted herself into the group, making sure she wedged between he and Cate. Giles felt instantly wary.

When she was certain she commanded everyone's attention, she continued, "There's to be races today. Some of the horse sellers are eager to show off the quality of the horse flesh." She leaned forward conspiratorially. "I know we can't expect the quality of the thoroughbreds we're used to watching at Epsom or Newmarket, but still the thought of races adds some excitement to the day." Candice turned to Cate. "Especially some excitement for you."

Giles saw a dangerous spark light Cate's green eyes. "Why would that be, Lady Fox-Haughton?" Her innocent tone boded ill for Candice. He wondered if Candice was aware of the pot she stirred.

The slight jerk of Candice's head indicated she was taken back by the directness of Cate's question, but she only hesitated for a moment. Her tone was pointed and left no room for misinterpretation. "Because I am sure you don't get any such entertainments being tucked away in the remote countryside as you are."

The message was catty and clear, with no retort that wouldn't be outright provoking. For an awful moment,

Giles feared Cate would not exercise restraint but Isabella intervened with a well-placed comment and averted disaster.

"Are we ready to look at ribbons? I can't eat another bite."

There was no shaking Candice after that. Instead of spending the afternoon with some of her female contemporaries who had been invited to the party, Candice insinuated herself into the ranks of Giles's friends. Technically, Giles could not fault her. She was his hostess, and it was assumed here as it was in London that they were together.

She was putting that assumption on full display today, Giles noted grimly as she doggedly clung to his right arm, leaving Cate to become uncomfortably aware of the odd number of women to men in their little group. But Candice's petty victory was short-lived. Giles smiled to see that Cate refused to be intimidated by such maneuvering. His grin widened when Tristan deftly moved in to offer his free arm to Cate, who declined it with a laugh.

"La! Moreland, you're the devil to think to steal me away from right under my cousin's nose!" She used the opportunity to link her arm through Giles's left, much to Candice's chagrin.

Giles joined in with her jest. "It's a good thing a man's got two arms when there's so many pretty women around."

Outwardly they made a gay party, going from stall to stall and exclaiming over the gewgaws on display, some ranging from a milkmaid's cheap fripperies to luxury items all the way from France brought to the fair particularly to catch the eye of a gentleman with means to afford such quality.

On Cecile's recommendation, they bought cakes of French milled soap. Giles had found it easy to purchase the soap for his cousin, although he had not found it easy to fathom the expression in her eyes when he'd handed her the cakes, neatly wrapped in a square of white cloth and tied with a lilac-colored ribbon.

At the ribbon stall, Cecile held up a narrow satin length of cherry-colored ribbon. "There, it would be perfect woven through your hair," she said to Cate. "Do persuade her, Giles. It would be perfect for the ball tomorrow night."

The dratted ball to close the house party. He hadn't wanted one but Candice had insisted that an entertainment of this level would be incomplete without one. Now it would be an exceedingly clumsy affair dancing attendance, no humor intended, on his supposed cousin and the jealous Candice.

"Cecile is right, you simply must have it." Giles confirmed, reaching to hand the vendor the required coins.

"No, I couldn't possibly accept it!" Cate protested. "The soap is gift enough."

Was that the beginnings of a blush on her cheeks? She'd been remarkably self-assured the entire afternoon, even in the wake of Candice's put-down. Giles exerted his considerable charm. "I will brook no refusal on this, dear cousin. Soap will eventually melt away but ribbon will last longer as a memento." He was conscious of the hard stare Candice gave him, but he did not waver his gaze from Cate to return it.

They approached the line of horse stalls, and Giles felt the tension growing on both sides of him; Candice waiting for the right opportunity to pounce, and Cate waiting to strike back. They'd become predatory animals, each stalking the other, and Giles didn't like the sensation it raised in him. He was quite aware that he was the prize in this hunt.

"I think either the sorrel mare or this brown are your best choices," Alain told his wife. "Was there another horse that caught your eye?" He asked when Cecile didn't immediately respond.

"What about that one?" Cecile pointed to a chestnut gelding further down the line. The horse was stocky, maybe fourteen hands high, not much bigger than a pony, with a broad chest. His smaller size was thoroughly pronounced against the larger stature of the other horses surrounding him. Additionally, his face looked forlorn, and when he turned his big brown horsey eyes their direction, Alain groaned.

"You are too softhearted, my dear. That horse is appealing to your emotions." Nonetheless, the group moved towards the gelding to take a closer look. Alain grabbed the bridle and pulled back the horse's lips to see his teeth while Tristan checked the legs.

"Cecile, darling," Candice gave a superior drawl while the men looked over the horse. "You can't possibly want this one. It's docile enough because it's practically dead. The others are much better choices. They've been bred to be a lady's mount. This one has fallen into it simply by accident."

Giles barely suppressed a moan. Of the group, Cecile knew the least about horseflesh on account that she'd been raised by a poor violin maker in France before meeting Alain. Riding and horses was something very new to her since their marriage. Candice had made Cecile's ignorance very clear with her thoughtless comment. If she wasn't careful, Alain would take her head off without compunction.

Cate stirred at his side. That was unless Cate got to her first. Cate stepped forward and studied the horse close up, bending to run a hand across the width of its chest.

"I suppose if your heart is set on it," Alain began, returning to Cecile's side. "There's nothing fundamentally wrong with the horse."

"Nothing wrong!" Candice exclaimed. "Wickham, you must persuade her to purchase a different mount. It is not at all suitable."

Giles cringed, not bothering to hide his disapproval of Candice's conduct. His friends were right, he would do well to sever his relationship with her now that she'd shown her true colors.

Cate straightened from her inspection, which had moved to the horse's withers. "Baron Wickham is right. There's nothing fundamentally wrong with the horse." She ducked under the rope in fluid motion and took up her spot on Giles's left. "However, I think the price is too much. You would do better to buy the horse after the races when the day is winding down and the vendors are more keen to sell. If the horse is not worth it, the price will come down. If the horse is quality, the price may go up. It's a risk but at least if the price goes up, you'll know the horse is worth something."

"I bow to your wisdom, Lady Cate," Alain said. "Let us find a place in the stands to watch the races since they are set to begin in a few minutes."

There was much activity surrounding the makeshift racetrack as they approached. People were laying odds on horses and others milled about looking at the entries. Giles handed Candice up into the stands and turned to assist Cate.

"I need a few moments of privacy," Cate whispered. "I'll be back."

Assuming she meant to seek out a ladies' convenience, Giles nodded and sat down next to Candice. To assure her safety and direction, he followed Cate with his eyes until she was out of view.

Once out of sight of the stands, Cate doubled back around to the stall where Cecile had seen the dark gelding. She took off her wide-brimmed hat and shook her hair free of its pins.

"Hello, Donovan."

The barrel-chested man at the stall looked up, recognition dawning on his tanned face. "Caterina, I thought that might have been you but I couldn't tell with that hat. It didn't make sense you would be all those coves. What are you doing?" He crossed the rope barrier and enveloped her in a big hug.

"It's too complicated to explain." Cate shook her head at her long-time friend. "Are you really selling King Charles here?" She motioned toward the horse, who like the king he was named for, was shorter in stature than most horses of his ilk.

The man looked at the ground, dismayed. "Times are tough, too tough. He's a good horse although the stubborn old fella is putting on a good show with all his acting today. I can't afford to keep him and some of the others. I'm only keeping the ones I can breed."

"But you can race him. He's still fast enough for these pony fairs. Surely, his winnings are worth his keep," Cate argued.

"That won't last forever and then where will I be with a horse that's too old for anything? In the meanwhile, he might pull up lame. These fair races are not organized affairs."

Cate nodded in agreement. She knew from experience just how unorthodox these events could be. She'd ridden in plenty. The life of a gypsy ebbed and flowed with the cycle of horse fairs throughout the English countryside.

"What's turning in your head, missy? I can see you have a plan," Donovan said, his own eyes sparking at the thought of a game.

"Can I ride King Charles today? I've seen the other horses. They're nothing special, just steady quarter horses. They look a lot better than Charlie so the odds on him will go way up. You can keep the winnings, and I can guarantee a solid sale after the race."

"Not to that snippy broad that was with you," Donovan protested.

"Oh no, but definitely to spite her." Cate laughed.

In truth, she'd had all she was going to take from the uppity Fox-Haughton woman, she thought, hurriedly stripping out of Lady Isabella's striped muslin and into the spare riding breeches and shirt Donovan carried in his trunk. All afternoon the woman had done her best to remind everyone of her place beside Giles. Interestingly enough, Giles seemed to begrudge her that position. Yet, gentleman that he was, he had done nothing to overtly dissuade her of the notion.

The last straw had been her callous assessment of King Charles. That horse was all heart, so attuned to his rider's feelings that he was practically human. She'd ridden him on a few occasions and knew him to be a mount that would do well with an experienced rider or with someone of Cecile's limited abilities.

She tucked her hair up into Donovan's borrowed cap as best she could without the requisite pins and bloused out the overlarge shirt to hide the hint of breasts beneath. Then she swung up onto King Charles and headed him toward the starting line with a wink for Donovan.

"Look, it's my gelding!" Cecile cried, tugging at Alain's sleeve excitedly.

Giles smiled over at her, taking in her enthusiasm and trying to put aside his growing concern that Cate had not returned. But since the races were about to start, there was little he could do in way of searching for her. Most likely, she'd been held up by the crowd.

"Lay a wager for me, Alain." Cecile beamed up at her husband. "The gelding to win."

"Are you sure?" Alain seemed dubious. "To win? That means he has to come in first. Why not to come in second or third?"

"My dear, it would be like throwing money away," Candice spoke around Giles in her patronizing tone.

Isabella broke away from her intense scrutiny of the horses as they lined up. She looked straight at Candice. "I'm in. The gelding to win. Tristan, place a bet for me and one for Lady Cate. She'll be glad to know when she returns that she has profited in her absence. I think I'll also lay a wager with you, Lady Fox-Haughton. Shall we have a quiet bet on the side between us? Say twenty pounds?"

"If you insist on throwing away good money, I am happy to take it," Candice replied with a tight smile.

"Very good." Isabella returned her attention to the starting line with a knowing smile creasing her lips.

The starting gun went off. The horses bolted in a haphazard manner from the line. The race would be two laps around the dirt track. Cecile's gelding managed to stay in the middle of the pack most of the first lap. Giles was impressed it could manage that much. Certainly Alain's assessment was correct—nothing was wrong with the horse, but it hadn't looked as if it had much zest for something as taxing as a race over rough terrain.

He had to give the rider his due. Whoever was riding

that horse had a splendid seat and an excellent command of the reins. Giles narrowed his gaze, studying the rider—long-legged and slim-waisted from the look of things. Graceful and elegant were two words that came to mind—not usually words he associated with male riders but words he'd often associated with Isabella's riding over the years.

As the pack passed the stands at the end of the first lap, the horse edged up to join the two horses attempting to break away from the group. Giles's estimation of both horse and rider rose. As they sped by, he caught a flash of cherry ribbon against the neck of the rider's white shirt. A dangerous suspicion began to loom in his mind. Suddenly, he knew why Cate hadn't come back from the privy.

By the last half, the race had been narrowed down to the gelding and one other. Cecile rose, cheering beside him. He rose too, his heart in his throat. If it was Cate and she was discovered, there'd be the devil to pay. Anger and worry warred within. Concerns for her safety competed with his anger that she would risk exposure after they'd agreed in the curricle that morning that the best way forward for both of them was discretion.

At the last, the gelding gave a spurt of speed and crossed the finish line by a decisive neck. It was not a large win but it was a clear win. Cecile and Isabella hugged each other in glee, while Isabella tossed Candice an "I told you so" smile and collected her winnings.

If Giles hadn't been so well bred, he would have laughed. As it was, he had enough to worry about.

"Spelthorne, I have a headache coming on. I must insist on returning to the abbey immediately so I can lie down. Will you mind terribly, taking me back in your curricle ahead of the others?" Candice pleaded.

Trapped, Giles had to acquiesce. She was his hostess, at least for now. He cast a look at Alain. "Make sure you find my cousin and that she gets back safely. I know the landau will be crowded with five," he said apologetically.

"Not to worry, Giles. It looks like we'll be buying a horse. I can ride home on it." Alain laughed good-naturedly as he handed the ladies down to the ground and set off to claim Cecile's horse.

Giles handed Candice into the curricle and settled beside her, glad to be away from the fair and on his way home. The day had been full of tension. The drive home would prove quiet and uneventful. He knew Candice. She would sit there and stew, nursing her supposed headache. He didn't really believe she had one. Candice had the constitution of an ox. She could sulk. He would drive and enjoy the peace.

They hadn't gone more than a mile, the pennants of the fair barely hidden from view behind them when Giles realized there would be no peace.

Candice stiffened beside him, preparing to speak. "Spelthorne, you've got five miles to start explaining why you're trying to pass off that tart as a shirttail relative. Anyone of breeding can see she's no lady. The dress is probably borrowed. It reeks of Lady Gresham's style."

"Madame, I think you go too far. In three sentences

you've managed to malign my cousin and my dear friend," Giles said coldly, hoping to freeze her inquisition with the voice of authority.

"Oh no, Spelthorne, if anyone went too far, it was you last night. I saw her leaving your private rooms, and I noted that her feet were bare—no doubt to try and hide the sound of her departure."

She knew. Giles stifled a groan. Oh God. There was going to be hell to pay.

Chapter Six

In the end, Giles was one guest short at supper that evening. After hearing the explanation, which even to him sounded a bit on the lame side of things, Lady Fox-Haughton repaired to her rooms, packed her trunks and left for London posthaste to make the most of the fading daylight for the short trip back into town. All in all, Giles thought supper and the ensuing evening of cards was the merrier for her absence.

While she claimed she left on moral grounds, Giles saw through the transparent claim to her real agenda; she wanted to unsettle the house party by depriving him of the needed numbers and a hostess to oversee the remaining activities. Giles foiled her ploy decisively. Isabella, who was a reigning London hostess of equal caliber to Candice, deftly stepped in to manage the ball for the following night and 'Lady Cate,' who Candice had obviously overlooked when planning her decampment, equaled out the numbers perfectly, slipping into Candice's vacancy and allowing Giles to sit out the card games. He used the opportunity to circulate among his guests, ensuring their good time.

By 11:00 and the arrival of the tea cart which signaled the end of the evening, Giles had discreetly dealt with all possible loose ends in regards to the day's events except one—he had yet to confront Cate about her risky display at the fair. There was no sense in putting it off and there would be no better time to do it than now unless he wanted to risk a trip to her rooms.

Seeing that Isabella was managing the tea, Giles scanned the room for Cate. Finding her in conversation with Alain and Cecile, he started towards them.

Cate felt him coming before she saw him begin the trip across the room to her side. She had the uncomfortable feeling of being watched, stalked. When she looked away from Alain and Cecile, she saw him searching for and finding her. Their eyes locked for an instant before she tore her gaze away and turned back to Cecile and Alain, animating her conversation with a false gaiety.

She felt "stalked" because of the guilt. After the euphoria of being victorious with King Charles, she'd been swamped with guilt. She had told Giles she'd be discreet during her time at the abbey but racing King Charles had been an act of flagrant disregard for discretion. What if someone had recognized her as Lady

Cate, Giles's cousin? What if Giles himself had recognized her? He might rethink their arrangement and toss her out of the abbey.

She'd told herself no one could possibly recognize her as she hastily changed back into her borrowed gown. But that fantasy was short-lived, quashed by Isabella as they piled into the landau for the journey home. Isabella had leaned forward and squeezed her hand, congratulating her on the victory. By that, Cate knew Isabella was referring to the horse race but also to the routing of Lady Fox-Haughton, who in a moment of pique upon seeing the gelding she'd declared useless, had demanded Giles escort her home immediately.

Horrified over her disguise being detected, Cate had asked how she'd known. Isabella smiled and made a small gesture to her hair. Cate knew at once Isabella meant the cherry ribbon. She'd felt her hair come down from beneath her cap during the race.

Now she was worried that Giles knew too. He'd been polite all evening, and she'd been relieved to hear that Lady Fox-Haughton had been called away suddenly to take care of matters in London. Everyone had accepted it as a plausible explanation for her absence. Still, whenever Giles had looked at her that evening, there'd been something predatory in his eyes, something that warned she had not fooled him. She was his quarry and there would be a reckoning.

The reckoning stood next to her, immaculate in dark evening attire and a subdued waistcoat done in burnished red the color of autumn leaves. "If you will excuse us, there is something I wish to show my cousin." He nodded to Alain and Cecile, and Cate found herself swiftly detached from the safety of their company with Giles's hand at her elbow.

"Are you enjoying yourself?" he inquired, sounding genuinely solicitous as he steered her towards the open doors leading to the verandah. It was no secret where he was taking her. Neither was there any reason to disguise their destination. There was absolutely nothing wrong with cousins stepping outside to view the gardens. Once out there, they would be visible to the guests inside although their conversation would not be overheard.

"I am enjoying myself as well as can be expected, considering the circumstances," Cate said, passing through the open doorway in front of Giles.

They stood for a few moments at the stone balustrade, appreciating the beauty of the lawn laid before them in the early fall moonlight. In the distance, she caught the burble of a fountain. She took a deep breath. "The lawn is lovely this time of night, but I suspect that is not the reason you brought me out here."

"No, it is not. It appears that you and I have different understandings of what *discretion* means. For instance, I believe discretion includes such behavior as making oneself as unobtrusive as possible. You, on the other hand, seem to believe discretion includes behaviors such as donning men's breeches and riding a horse in a fair race on an ungroomed track."

Cate fought back a smile. He was getting worked up now. "I didn't mean for you to find out." She said in defense of her actions.

He quirked an eyebrow. "Do you think it was only a bad idea because I found out? That it would have been a good idea if I hadn't known? That's rather poor ethics. It shouldn't have been done at all. Any type of harm could have befallen you."

He had been concerned for her. The thought sent a warm sensation through her. In spite of the circumstances, he'd been concerned for her well-being. It was the second time he'd shown such concern that day, the first being his thoughtfulness over her need for clothing.

Cate tried to reciprocate. "I didn't do it to provoke you," she uttered softly. "I did it to provoke *her*. She was entirely out of line and needed to be put in her place."

Giles leaned on the balustrade and harrumphed. "Normally, I'd agree but I'd rather not have her as an enemy when the winter season starts and parliament's in session."

"Perhaps you should have persuaded her to stay then. She could be a powerful ally to help you obliterate my claim." Cate saw with the astute clarity she reserved for fortune-telling what it had cost Giles to give the woman up, distasteful as she was.

"Oh, yes. She's an ambitious woman. Her political aspirations were stifled after the death of her first husband. It seemed she thought I'd be perfect for molding into the next prime minister. I suppose that avenue's closed to me now." He gave a self-deprecating snort to indicate how little he cared for that loss. "Still, I feel compelled to warn you, if she gets scent of your claim to legitimacy, or discovers I don't have any fourth cousins on my mother's side, she'll annihilate you."

"Why would you warn me? Wouldn't you want that?" Cate asked, turning to look at Giles's profile, strong and leonine in the spill of light coming from the drawing room.

"It's not honorable to feed the unsuspecting to the wolves," he replied without equivocation.

"Even if the unsuspecting person in question lays claim to your domain?" Cate whispered, hardly daring to breath.

"Even if," Giles said solemnly. "Ethics and honor don't mean much if they are applied haphazardly simply to gain one's benefit."

Cate thought there might be a message hidden in the statement just for her. But she could not quite decipher it any more than she could decipher the darkening depths of his eyes. There was a sadness mirrored in them that she did not comprehend.

He lifted a hand and gently stroked her cheek, a half-smile playing at his mouth. "You're an interesting woman, Cate. I would have liked to have known you," Giles paused for a moment and then added softly, "without."

Without.

The word quivered in the air between them, burgeoning with untold meaning. She knew what he meant—without the complexities of the situation surrounding them. But what did it mean? Did it mean that he liked her? That she could have had Spelthorne and him without attacking his heritage? She searched his eyes for confirmation of his thoughts but the vulnerable moment had passed. He was all business again.

"You will attend the ball tomorrow night. I am certain Isabella will have something suitable for you to borrow. It is, after all, only a country ball and gowns don't have to be as elaborate as in town. Sleep well." He bowed briskly and took himself back into the drawing room where the tea was finished and the guests were preparing to retire to their rooms.

Cate stayed on the verandah, enjoying the opportunity to watch him from a distance. She had never met a man of his ilk before, so committed to his sense of right and wrong that he would not be tempted to stray from his code, even when his very identity was on the line. She had glimpsed a part of who he was beyond the handsome façade and found the core of him as attractive as the outer layers he showed to the world.

She replayed the conversation in her mind, savoring the insights, the kind words, the touch of his hand on her cheek. She could hear the sound of his voice just as surely as if he stood there saying the words she treasured, "I wish I could have known you. Without."

"Rubbish!" Magda declared firmly, helping Cate out of her dinner gown while Cate relayed the events of the evening. "That's what he wants you to think. He's trying to soften you up, talk you into dropping your claims." She shook her head. "Men will promise a woman anything and when they have what they want, they'll take back their word."

Cate turned from the long mirror to face Magda. "Other men, maybe. Not Giles. He's different." The intensity of her defense startled even her.

Magda threw up her hands. "It's been one day and already he's charmed you. He's no different than his father, I tell you. Celeste was swept off her feet during the courtship and then dumped here in the country, forgotten entirely. You should know better. You've read the diary. Like father like son," she warned.

"But he's not his father's son, literally." Cate shrugged into a satin wrapper and belted it at the waist. Magda's warning left her deflated. She crossed the room to the window seat where she'd spent the previous night. She knew herself to be a shrewd woman who understood human nature. She'd seen enough of the good and the bad through her years of telling fortunes. She could indeed read people like books, usually without error. Had she been so wrong about Giles?

"There, there, my sweetling," Magda perched on the edge of the bed, her tone not as condemning. "I know you don't want to believe me. Don't take my word for it. Test your thoughts. Tell me everything that happened when you left for the fair this morning."

Cate brightened at the prospect and shifted around in the window seat to get comfortable. "Giles took me up in the curricle next to him so we could talk about our strategy, about our mutual need for discretion. I took it as a good sign. He was not going to dismiss me out of hand. We would explore the possibilities of my claim together.

"He made sure I could avoid the company of that odious Fox-Haughton woman by seeing me attached to Lady Isabella and Lady Cecile. After lunch we all went shopping together, and he bought me a cake of French milled soap. He squired me about all afternoon." She paused, leaving out the bit about the races. "I am certain we would have driven back in the curricle together if Lady Fox-Haughton hadn't come down with a headache. He treated me as if I were one of them, as if I belonged in their circles. Not once did he imply I was less than worthy of their company. We mustn't forget all his kindnesses this morning with the gowns." Cate finished her recitation of Giles's good deeds, feeling confident that Magda would have to secede some of her harsh position.

Magda fiddled with the pale-blue counterpane, tracing its patterns with a finger. "Have you thought why a gentleman would go to such lengths for a stranger? For a woman he does not know and who is not of his class? More to the point, why would a gentleman do such things for a woman who has the means to depose him from his life of luxury?"

Cate looked squarely at Magda. "Because he is a good man."

Magda snorted. "You're half right. He's a man. Can you not think of another reason? One that has more logic?"

"No, I cannot, but I am sure you can. What do you think?" Cate said testily from the window seat. Magda's pragmatism was becoming difficult to stomach, but she'd been right about much in Cate's life and she was the only mother figure Cate had known. Difficult or not, it was hard to turn away from Magda's counsel.

"He wanted to show you a slice of his life and how ill-equipped you are to assume a place in such circles." Magda held up her fingers. "First, the gowns. He sent enough of them to impress you with their fine tailoring and to swamp you with choices he knew you couldn't make between a carriage gown or a walking dress. The clothes were meant to intimidate you. Second, he imposed on you a new name and a false identity because he is embarrassed by your presence, not because he wants to assimilate you into the house party. Third, he kept you to himself because he doesn't want you out his sight. You're too dangerous left on the loose. Fourth, he bought you an effortless gewgaw—your precious soap and ribbons—to show you how much you lacked. You could not even afford one of those items on a whim. Are you charmed now with your handsome prince? Should I go on to examine the motives behind his facile words on the verandah this evening?"

Cate swallowed hard. Magda's logic seemed far more reasonable than her own quickly paling assumptions. She had no proof to counter Magda's claims beyond her intuition. Deep down in her heart, she knew Giles was not as manipulative as Magda suspected. Protective of his domain? Yes. Willing to fight her for

it? Most definitely. But he would not fight unfairly.
There was nothing to tell Magda. So she drew her knees
up and wrapped her arms about them and enjoyed the
pastoral night view from her window.

After a length of silence, she heard Magda rise from
the bed and putter about the room, picking up clothes
and tidying. "I don't mean to hurt your feelings," she
muttered.

Cate sighed, balancing her chin on her knees. "I know."

"Where do we go from here?" Magda asked, after
another long pause.

Cate was surprised by the question. Up until now,
Magda had planned everything, from when they
launched their campaign to how they would gain a
foothold in the house. Of course Cate herself had had to
execute the plans.

Now, Cate realized, Magda didn't have the information she had. Magda wasn't privy to the details about
the curate.

"We stay. He's sent for the curate. It will take a bit,
maybe a month, for the curate to travel down. His parish
is up in the north, outside of York. Then we shall see
what is necessary to secure our claim."

That news seemed to please Magda. "A month of
soft living. Good beds, hot food. It's a start."

Cate seized the moment. She was going to be in
charge here. She needed to assert herself, something she
didn't hesitate to do except with Magda. It was time to
change that. "Yes, we have a month of good living
ahead of us. I intend to use it to full advantage and enjoy

the opportunities available, starting tomorrow. I'm going to the ball as Lady Cate Winthrop, and I'm going to have a good time," she said firmly. "Moreover, I am going to extend to Giles the courtesy he has extended to me and behave civilly in his company. I hope that by doing so he'll see my claim to Spelthorne as something other than an act of revenge or anger at being cheated out of a birthright."

Magda paused in the doorway to the dressing room. "Very well, have your fantasy of playing lady of the manor but don't forget who you are and what you're about when the time comes for the fantasy to be over. Spelthorne has bought himself some time by deciding to send for the curate. This gives him a month to gather his resources and to plot. You must remember that always."

"He's not the only one who's been bought time. We have too. We need that time just as desperately."

Alone in his study, Giles idly flipped through a calendar. He had one month to uncover additional support regarding his heritage. The curate-cum-vicar would be a source of evidence when he arrived but Giles wanted more.

Tristan and Alain had offered to stay up with him and talk but he'd declined, preferring solitude to assess his thoughts—thoughts which were filled with intriguing images of the day just spent. To be sure, the day had been fraught with a certain tension. He'd had to make Cate's masquerade believable while mitigating Candice's inquiries and sharp tongue.

Surprisingly, there had also been pleasure in the day. There had been the moment when he'd spied Cate on the landing coming down to join the throng that morning. He'd been captivated by the sight of her for long moments before he recalled who she was and reminded himself why she was there. She'd looked elegant and composed in the borrowed muslin and her hair twisted up underneath her hat. She'd looked as if she belonged among them.

There had been the gaiety of shopping through the booths and a glimpse of Cate's steely backbone. Remembering how she'd claimed a place at his side, undaunted by Candice's possessiveness still brought a smile to his face. He could feel it spreading across his mouth, and he chuckled to himself. It had been an easy thing to spend money on her at the fair. The unfettered delight and surprise at receiving the soap and ribbons had thrilled him.

He'd bought Candice a ruby bracelet once, and she'd politely thanked him with no more genuine warmth than if he'd brought her a posy of violets. He would wager Cate would have been just as thrilled with violets as she had been with soap.

Wagering conjured up the last image of the fair. He had scolded her on the terrace for her rash actions but if the situation between them had been more amicable, he doubted he would have cared beyond concern for her safety. In truth, he had little concern there. She'd shown herself to be nearly nonpareil as a rider. She'd easily keep up with him and his horse-mad friends.

He'd almost thought he was mistaken about the race when he saw her again at dinner. It was hard to reconcile the serene, neatly coiffed woman seated at supper in a pale-blue gown of eau de nil silk with the reckless hoyden from the track.

He had to remind himself that looks didn't make a lady. There was more to it than looking pretty in fancy gowns, but he had to admit she had the bearing for it. So far she'd pulled off her part of the masquerade quite successfully, as long as one didn't talk to her too long and realize her conversation was not all it should be. He'd noticed today, she was a quick study. By mid-afternoon, she'd picked up on one of Isabella's favorite expressions, "La." He'd been neatly surprised to hear her use it when dealing with Candice.

Watching Cate had definitely proved entertaining and insightful today. He hadn't uncovered anything today about supporting his own claim to Spelthorne, but he had learned several things about her. After watching men in parliament and assessing the people and issues that came before him as the earl, Giles thought himself to be a good judge of human nature. What he had seen of Cate, her strength, her tenacity, her own sense of justice, suggested to him that she was serious about her claim to Spelthorne. She believed in the truth of that claim. She was not out to scam him but to lay claim to what was rightfully hers.

Because of that, he found her to be an intoxicating mix of danger and desire. He admired many of the qualities she'd shown him today.

He'd meant it, as foolish as the statement may have been, on the verandah when he'd said he wished he could have known Cate without the quagmire surrounding them. He doubted the resolution of the pending issue between them would leave much room for friendship, especially since it could only be resolved one way—in his favor.

However, he did have a month before the curate arrived. One month in which he must discreetly gather evidence in his cause. Yet, still a month when the issue between them was somewhat stalemated. The idea grew in his mind. It was just possible that the month could be used for something in addition to evidence gathering. He could spend it with Cate, the person.

But to what end? His practical nature queried. What could come of that endeavor? His practical nature would need an answer beyond the mere whimsy of wanting to know her, to be near her, to watch and see what kind of crazy stunt she'd pull next.

He hit upon an answer that would satisfy his practical self. He would get her ready for her new life, one that he would fund when her claims were dismissed. When that happened, she would need somewhere to go. She would not be going back to life with the Rom. She had left her caravan, the only source of home she'd likely ever known. She would be devastated when the claims were proven false. Some funds would soften the blow.

He'd see her able to purchase a decent home in the country and provided with a modest allowance for living. He would set her up as country gentry and for that, she'd need some training. She would need to know how to order dresses, what to wear to certain functions, how to run a small household, and myriad other items. Over the course of the month, he'd teach her those things. He would organize her new life for her.

Ah yes. His practical side was very pleased with his answer.

Chapter Seven

By 7:00 the next evening, Cate was nearly shaking with nerves and anticipation while she sat in her room, waiting to be summoned. She was going to a real ball with gentry and even a few peers in attendance. It was just as she imagined that evening in the Denbigh's garden. Giles would be there. He would see her in the lovely gown of rose crepe with its vandyked flounces at the hem showing off the delicate cream silk underskirt beneath. Her hair was done to suit her long-ago fairy tale, piled high on her head with a few gentle curls allowed to stray, framing her face. Throughout the carefully piled coiffure was wound a subtle strand of small pearls, courtesy of Isabella, who had apologized they were only Scottish pearls.

Cate wiggled her toes in the satin dancing slippers of

pale cream, another item on loan from Isabella's seemingly endless trunk of clothing. They were a bit too large, a subtle reminder that the reality fell short from the imaginings of her mind. The dress was borrowed. It wasn't the aquamarine gown she dreamed of wearing and, like all of Isabella's loaned garments, it had to be hemmed before it fit Cate well enough. The shoes were stuffed with wads of cotton in the toes to prevent her from tripping, although she hoped she didn't have to move around overly much. That was another concern contributing to her rising nerves as she waited. In her daydreams, she knew how to dance properly—not the wild abandoned dances she performed so well at the gypsy camp.

The knock came, summoning her to join the house-guests downstairs to mingle with the guests arriving from neighboring homes before the dancing began. Cate rose from her place at the window seat and smoothed her skirts once more, squared her shoulders and raised her chin, doing her best to glide across the floor and glad that she'd sent Magda below stairs earlier so that the woman couldn't see her "putting on airs."

Cate opened the door, expecting to see a maid. She had not expected to see Giles. He was the host, after all, and, had myriad responsibilities. Yet there he was, resplendent in dark evening clothes, his hair combed to burnished perfection, not an inch of him askew from what appeared to be a very complicated knot in his cravat to the neatly pressed line of his evening trousers.

Cate blushed. She was sure real ladies didn't stare in such an obvious manner. She hadn't been able to help herself. He looked entirely magnificent.

"Are you ready to go down?" Giles asked, either unaware of what she'd been doing or showing his impeccable manners yet again by overlooking her blunder.

"Yes. I don't suppose I can be any readier. The longer I wait, the more nervous I'll get."

"You look splendid. There's no need to be nervous. The other ladies who opted to take dinner trays in their rooms and rest before the entertainment are just starting to come down as well." Giles offered his arm to her and Cate, after two days in his company, easily took it, laying her white-gloved arm on his right sleeve.

He covered her hand briefly with his left and whispered, "Remember, this isn't London. It's merely a country ball, much less formal, although I daresay it's likely to be rowdier. You will do fine."

His sincere encouragement caused Cate to hazard a sideways glance up at him while they walked down the long stretch of hall to the main staircase. "Why are you being so nice? You don't have to be. I hardly think I'd be as polite if I were in your situation."

"First, Cate, let me be clear. I am not *in* any situation. I am the Earl of Spelthorne, and I will remain so. If it is anyone who is in a situation, it is you. Your claims will come to naught. However, I am intrigued by you. I made it clear that I would have liked to have met you without these entanglements. There is nothing we can do about your situation until the vicar arrives, so why not enjoy the opportunity? With the right guidance, I am sure you will find the experience enriching."

A dozen retorts vied for the right to be heard on her tongue. Did he know how arrogant he sounded? She didn't dare tell Magda for fear of the older woman having the chance to say "I told you so." She might have given free rein to the retorts if his one thought hadn't paralleled hers so nearly. Why not enjoy the hiatus between her claims and the vicar arriving?

"I suppose there's no harm in playing Cinderella for a bit," she said, hoping he realized how lucky he was to get off so lightly for his high-handed behavior, but realizing he probably had no idea.

They were nearing the staircase. Giles chuckled at her reference. "Cinderella? When I think of you, I think of Snow White." Cate felt the weight of his stare on her and felt her body grow warm. Her usually glib tongue could not think of anything witty with which to respond.

Giles covered the silence with a witty response. "Well, Cinderella is probably appropriate for tonight. It is a ball, and you'll get to dance with some nicely established men, although I doubt any of them will turn out to be Prince Charming. We're all remarkably normal folk around these parts."

They had come to the top of the stairs and Cate looked down into the throng below. She gasped. "Remarkably normal" had nothing to do with the hall below her or the glimpses she could catch of the drawing room-cum-ballroom through the flower-festooned archway beyond.

Sometime between the group of guests returning home

from a day of hiking around nearby follies and the supper hour, the hall had been transformed into an indoor garden complete with low stone benches, topiary trees planted in large urns and cut into spiraling shapes, lanterns placed about the entry to give it the look of a lit garden at night and she even heard the tinkling of a fountain—a genuine fountain at the center of the hall.

Giles leaned forward towards her ear and whispered, "Champagne."

At first she didn't understand the reference. What did champagne have to do with the fountain? Then she noticed guests dipping goblets into the streams of liquid, noticed the golden hue of the "water." Her eyes widened at such invention.

"Not as fancy as London?" She turned to Giles and raised a doubting eyebrow. "I can hardly imagine how this could be surpassed.

They neared Isabella, where she and Tristan stood greeting the guests near the arched doorway leading into the drawing room. Upon closer inspection, Cate could see that the flowers garlanding the entrance were roses in all shades of pink and red. She had never seen so many roses in one place.

"Many of these are from Tristan's greenhouses," Isabella supplied, catching her attention. "Aren't they perfect for Giles's "Last Rose of Summer" ball?" She smiled, looking confident and lovely in the gauzy seafoam green confection she wore. "Your gown turned out well."

"Oh yes." Cate said, only just beginning to see why

Isabella had chosen the color for her. The lovely rose hue of the gown was the perfect foil for the room beyond the archway, ablaze with lights and filled with brass urns of floral arrangements featuring roses in the niches lining the walls.

At the far end of the ballroom, musicians began tuning up their instruments on the raised dais. Giles slipped a stiff piece of paper into her gloved hand. When she looked down, she discovered it to be none other than a dance card and, horror of horrors, it was filled in. Entirely. Not a blank slot was to be found. Casting a quick glance at Isabella, Cate noted she had looped the card about her wrist. Cate quickly followed suit and fumbled for a believable protest. "But I don't know any of these gentlemen."

"No need to know them," Giles said urbanely. "It would look amiss if my own cousin, no matter how far removed, was a wallflower at my party."

There was no chance for further protest. Giles was too busy organizing. "Cate, I'll need to leave you here in Gresham's capable hands. As hostess and as the highest ranking male present, Isabella and I need to lead off the dancing. Tristan will dance with you this first set."

Cate gaped at him in astonishment. For a man who remembered every last detail when it came to supplying her with clothing and accessories, could he truly have overlooked the likelihood that she didn't know how to dance in society? Her fairy tale was getting off to a rocky start. Cinderella had gone to the ball knowing how to waltz!

Swallowing her pride, Cate reached for Giles, trying to keep him from moving off before she could confess her lack of ability, but he was beyond her grasp, sailing toward the orchestra and the top of the ballroom with Isabella on his arm.

Slowly, she became alarmingly aware of Viscount Gresham at her elbow. His interrogating brown gaze seemed to know all in a glance. "A quadrille's not near as dreadful as a minuet. Thankfully those are becoming less and less the dance of choice for opening these affairs," he drawled, making no attempt to put her at ease like Giles had done or to befriend her as his wife had. It was no secret he held her in contempt. Anything he had done at the fair for her had been mostly for Giles's peace of mind.

"I find both the quadrille and the minuet insufferable." Cate opted for taking the high ground. Perhaps she could convince him she simply didn't care to dance.

He wasn't fooled. "A quadrille is easy enough to learn. It's just a collection of country dances when you break it down, nothing all that sophisticated really. Just watch the other couples." With that, the viscount took her by the elbow and insinuated them into a group forming near the door. The music started, they bowed and curtsied, and Cate discovered the viscount had been right.

There were things to be thankful for with the quadrille. They danced with three other couples, saving her from having to be in close proximity with the viscount and one didn't dance with any partner too long as to truly show their ineptitude. Afterwards, the viscount escorted her back to Giles's side, commenting in a low voice meant only for her, "One dance down, fourteen to go until the intermission." She was not naïve enough to take his parting sally as a sign of support. He meant it as an illustration of her lack of breeding. She read all that he meant to imply. Real ladies, even if they didn't dance effortlessly, knew the steps. How could she expect to claim Spelthorne when she couldn't manage a basic dance?

That fired her blood. She wasn't about to let his galling comment ruin an evening she'd waited a lifetime for. When her next partner came to claim her, she lifted her chin and let him sweep her onto the floor. This dance was a polka, and she fared better than she had with the quadrille. She quickly found that there were no expected figures or patterns and that her partner, the squire's son, was willing to throw himself into the fast-paced dance. Soon she was breathless and quite enjoying herself as he spun her about the floor.

The polka was followed by other gallops and other rowdy polkas and other men who seemed eager to dance with her. She knew she was succeeding with fitting in. They smiled with her, charmed and flirted. "How was it," they said, "that Giles had managed to keep such a lovely cousin hidden all these years?" Oh yes, she was succeeding.

The orchestra played a waltz, the first of the evening, and Cate didn't dare to push her luck. She convinced her partner, an older gentleman this time that she'd prefer to sit and sip a glass of champagne. He seemed all too happy to oblige. Cate suspected he too was feeling winded from all the energetic dancing.

There was another polka and then another waltz. Giles materialized at her side and this time there was no escape. "I believe it is finally my turn," he said, drawing her to her feet from the chaise where she sat chatting between sets with Cecile and Alain.

"I don't need to dance. I've danced all evening," she protested. To her credit, she had watched the dancers through the first waltz, trying to catalog their steps. The dance didn't appear to be overly complicated but it did appear to be overly intimate. With any of the other gentlemen she'd danced with that night, she would have been willing to try it. The intimate contact of hands on waists or hands nestled against the small of backs would have been pure mechanics with any of them. Not so with Giles. She doubted she would be able to concentrate on the new steps with Giles so close.

"One cannot attend a ball and not dance the waltz," he cajoled, although it was clear he wasn't looking for her assent. He had already decided she would dance with him; another fine example of his high-handed attempts to organize everyone around him. Of course, he knew she couldn't protest. Just as it would look awkward if his cousin had an empty dance card, it would look incredibly suspicious should his cousin refuse the courtesy of a waltz.

They joined the throng on the dance floor, mostly younger couples with stamina. "I must warn you—" she began as they positioned themselves, his hand at her back, feeling as warm and strong as she'd known it would.

"Ah yes." Giles smiled down at her. "Tristan told me. You can't dance, although you've been doing a credible job of faking it. Perhaps too credible. All your vivacity is quite noticeable. I thought we'd agreed you'd not call attention to yourself."

Cate felt the joy she'd garnered go out of the evening. "What is wrong with vivacity?"

The music started and Giles guided them down the floor with quick, expert movements.

"I was simply enjoying myself, no small feat after being put in an untenable position. One that I was put in on purpose, I might add," Cate challenged. "How dare you fill my dance card, when you must have suspected that I had no notion how to do any of these dances. Then you complain when I succeed in performing the role you laid out for me. Did you want me to fall on my face? Did you mean to humiliate me with my own ignorance? If so, I must inform you that you've failed dreadfully."

Giles whirled them through a corner, his pique showing in the jerky turn. "I did not set you up to fail. I am a man of honor," he ground out. "I may have overlooked the fact that you wouldn't know the dances, but you've shown yourself to be capable and a quick study. I merely wished to caution you against such lively dancing," he repeated.

The small orchestra began playing a second waltz to an Irish folk tune. "Ah, 'The Last Rose of Summer,' "

Giles said. "A very good selection before going into supper. Shall we sit down? Have you had enough waltzing?"

A spontaneous plan formed in her mind. A saucy smile quirked at her lips. "No. I find I like waltzing very much," Cate responded.

Giles pulled her back into the fray, and Cate took advantage of the moment to fit herself against his frame so that thighs touched thighs through the thin layers of her gown. Then she pushed the limits of his honor. She'd noted with earlier partners that gentlemen felt required to match their steps and pacing to that of their partners. Cate sped up, gradually pushing them both to a rapid whirl of turns and revolutions. It was an exhilarating battle—she trying to speed them up and Giles desperately attempting to keep them respectably sedate.

"I must tell you, Cate," Giles scolded as they fairly raced by another couple at the bottom turn, "that the woman is always in pursuit and that the male leads. He is responsible for setting the pace."

She snorted at that. How ridiculous and egocentric of men to place women in the position of "pursuit." "Are there no lengths a man will not go for the sake of flattering himself?"

"It is hardly a matter of ego. It is a matter of honor," Giles said curtly. "A woman is in the position of pursuit because it allows her to dance forward and remove the risk of tripping over her skirts."

Undaunted, Cate fired back, "A good reason for allowing women's dresses to be shorter. Then positions wouldn't matter unless of course such a requirement really was designed for promoting the male ego after all."

"Cate, I must insist that we slow down. We're drawing attention, and we must keep the appropriate distance." Giles's voice held a hint of warning that suggested he was not even remotely amused by her antics. "If you do not allow me to control our movements—"

"Then you'll do what?" Cate broke in, flashing a coy grin that teased, even as she urged him to greater speed and refused to give into the steely strength of his arm as he tried to readjust her position away from him. "I don't see what all the fuss is about. I find it much easier to dance closer anyway, especially if one is worried about tripping."

They swung past the doors leading out to the verandah, and Giles maneuvered them neatly into the darkness outdoors. Too late Cate knew intuitively she'd pushed him too far. His anger was palpable as he led them down the length of the verandah to a shadowed place where they wouldn't be noticed.

"Is all this a joke to you?" Giles began. "I talk of discretion and you constantly flaunt it. You make a mockery of my requests, you call attention to yourself in the most inappropriate fashion. I don't want my house-guests to leave tomorrow remembering my 'cousin.' However, after your performance tonight, it will be impossible for the male population to forget."

"You're quite the priggish scold, you know," Cate said coolly. "I will not be taken to task by a man who's a slave to propriety." She turned to walk back to the ballroom, determined to not let his blue mood sour the evening.

He grabbed her arm. "I am a man of honor who is bound by his gentlemanly obligations to offer you protection while you're under my roof, whether I like it or not. Are you curious to know why those men in there are not likely to forget you? Or do you already know?"

She said nothing, somewhat numbed by the ferocious warrior-lord who now replaced the carefully manicured gentleman. She thought she'd understood Giles Moncrief perfectly—a genteel, handsome, honorable man who had lived a soft life, faced with few worries or concerns, and consequently, a man ultimately lacking in intensity. She was beginning to see how wrong she was. His honor was not the soft spot she'd envisioned. It was his suit of armor and it was without a chink. She had been wrong about being able to exploit his gentlemanly code, and she began to worry over what else she might have been wrong about. Worse, if she'd been wrong, was Magda, with her cynical explanations, right?

"They think that your vivacious dancing is an invitation for certain attentions of a less gentlemanly nature. A lady is more circumspect with her dancing and is conscious of how she displays her virtue." His voice was at a low roar.

"Nonsense," Cate countered. "That is the most outlandish assumption I've heard. I was merely having a good time. Where I come from dancing is for celebration. It is an expression of joy. There are, of course, dances of a more seductive nature, but I have never engaged in them and I certainly did nothing more to-night than enjoy myself."

"I assure you, you did far more than enjoy yourself. It may have escaped your notice that the polka and the waltz are both closed dances, meaning they involve an embrace of one's partner. The polka is saved from scandalous repute because of its speed. However, the waltz is still considered by many to be shocking because of the amount of touching."

"Everyone was doing it. I don't see the fuss, Giles."

"No one was doing it your way. There are rules, Cate. For instance, there must be distance between the partners so that touching is reduced to the bare minimum." Exasperation rang in his voice, the secret language of dance clear to her now.

His explanations put an entirely different construction on her interactions with her other partners. She'd thought they were merely being warm, friendly. Now, she began to think differently.

She had not been successful tonight. She'd been foolish. Hot tears burned in her eyes. In the distance, she could hear the faint strains of a clock sounding the midnight hour and the bustle of people heading into the cold collation supper laid out in the refreshment room.

She couldn't go in there and, perhaps, it would be best if she didn't. She'd only cause Giles more embarrassment and herself as well. She was no better than she ought to be. But that was her private disappointment. She had a façade to maintain. She wouldn't let Giles see her cry.

Tonight was the proof that Magda had been right. He'd plotted to show her how wide the chasm was between her and the life she hoped to attain. She could put on a dress and thread her hair with pearls. She could even dance in the ballroom but it wasn't enough, not even close to enough. Actions and appearances masked hidden messages and nuances that she hadn't even begun to suspect lay beneath such harmless activities.

"I think I will excuse myself from the rest of the ball. It's midnight and the magic is over," she said bravely, refusing to apologize.

"I think that would be best. I'll make your excuses," Giles said stiffly, releasing her arm, letting her find her way circumspectly back to her room.

He had not meant to make her cry. He was fairly sure he'd caught a tell-tale catch in her voice. But he had to make her understand how precarious her presence here was. If he was to set her up in the country somewhere, she needed a clean reputation. Small hamlets and sleepy villages were unforgiving places for people of blemished character. It was imperative that he begin her education tomorrow as soon as the guests departed. There was much more she needed to know than what he'd anticipated. Seeing her tonight had shown him how much he took for granted in his world, a world he'd lived in since birth. Manners and social protocol were so thoroughly ingrained in him and yet she knew none of them—a sharp reminder of the contrast between his rarefied world and the world that lay beyond it.

Seeing her tonight had also been invigorating. She'd

been a breath of fresh air—no that was too cliché, too understated. She'd been a gust blowing through the ballroom, an exotic dervish. A secret part of himself that he dare not reveal had thrilled to the sight of her whirling about the ballroom, her dark hair coming down in tendrils, her face flushed with pleasure at her exertions. When she had teased him at the last, he'd itched to play the rake and take her challenge, giving into the impulse of waltzing with her in the same wild abandon.

Giles leaned on the balustrade and pressed his hands to his head. What was happening to him? One moment he was chastising Cate for inappropriate behavior, and the next he was longing for her in spite of those same behaviors.

He felt a movement beside him and smelled the familiar vanilla fragrance of a friend. He didn't need to look up to know Isabella stood beside him.

"Has she gone up to her chambers?" She asked quietly.

Giles nodded.

"I hope you weren't too hard on her. Perhaps she didn't understand the implications. Our worlds are very different from one another."

Giles looked up, brow furrowing with a question.

"After seeing her tonight, I thought I recognized her from somewhere. Tristan told me. Alain has told Cecile, just now." Isabella went on, a gentle hand on his sleeve, "You're bearing up admirably. You should know, we all think you've done the right thing by keeping her here until it can be resolved, although I know it must be most difficult on you. The four of us have made some decisions."

"Decisions?" Giles pressed, suddenly wary.

"Yes, we talked briefly and we've decided that we must stay with you until all is settled. The four of us are staying on after the guests leave tomorrow to help you in whatever way we can."

Giles felt himself smile in the darkness, tension ebbing from him at the prospect of having his friends near. It would indeed make the upcoming month, and whatever lay beyond it, easier to bear. He squeezed Isabella's gloved fingers. "Thank you. Let me tell you what I have planned." He went on to outline his plans for Cate's future, feeling relieved that now they all knew.

Isabella listened quietly. When he'd finished, she said, "Don't worry, Giles. We'll take care of everything just as you've taken care of everything for us for so many years. We are here for the duration."

Chapter Eight

The next day Cate learned that departing a house party was an event of its own. Guests had slept until the unthinkably late hour of 11:00 and then risen, dressed, and ate a leisurely breakfast either in their rooms, as many of the ladies chose to do, or in the breakfast parlor where Cate found herself so outnumbered by gentlemen that she quietly took her toast and tea out onto the back verandah.

Afterward, the laconic nature of the household instantly transformed into action as if by tacit agreement at precisely half past twelve, a barrage of servants would begin the arduous task of packing and carrying traveling trunks and bandboxes downstairs to the main hall.

Cate watched the growing piles of luggage in wide-eyed amazement from her inconspicuous post, in a small parlor off the main hall. The amount of clothing guests

125

had brought to a five-day house party was overwhelming. It was no wonder Isabella had dresses to spare. Cate doubted the caravan's entire wardrobe would have filled more than two of the large trunks being stacked in the hall. From there they would be loaded in the long line of conveyances waiting in the drive.

That was another point of revelation. Several guests had brought not one but two carriages with them; one for his or her own traveling pleasure and another to carry their servants where they would be organized into piles before being transported to the conveyances lining the drive.

Then there was the whole business of leave-taking. After the carriages were loaded with their cargo, the guests began the long parade out in an orderly fashion, which Cate was certain Giles had meticulously orchestrated so that no one was forced to sit in their carriage while awaiting the departure of someone ahead of them in line.

From her vantage point, she could glimpse Giles at the front door with Isabella and Tristan at his side, farewelling the guests, graciously accepting compliments, and promising to see everyone again in town at the Little Season in a few months when hunting season was over.

The words *Little Season* caused Cate to sit a bit straighter. She focused on Giles. For a man whose right to the title was being challenged, he looked supremely confident, the promises to meet again flowing easily from his lips. Either he was an accomplished actor, able to mask his feelings, or he truly wasn't concerned. The latter thought gave Cate pause. As the last carriage prepared to pull out of the drive, Cate was struck by the gravity of her situation, by how much protection the presence of the guests had afforded her.

With a house full of people, Giles had little time to do anything in relation to clearing his name or debunking her claims. With that obstacle gone, there was nothing preventing him from pursuing whatever course of action he wished to take. Perhaps he wasn't concerned because he had a veiled plan.

Cate thought of other things too. The warmth she'd felt from Isabella and Cecile right up to the ball last night had been absent this morning. Originally she'd accounted for the former's brusque tone when she'd poked her head into the parlor and seen Cate sitting there as nothing more than Isabella being busy with the departures.

Cecile had not left her rooms all day. That too Cate had attributed to the lateness of the ball. Now she was realizing neither lady had sent down any trunks. No carriages had been ordered to bear them away. The signs meant two things. First, the ladies and their formidable husbands were staying. Second, Cecile and Isabella knew why she was really there. Giles had stacked the deck.

The thoughts had barely registered when Isabella swept into the little parlor, looking marvelously elegant and composed in a cream-colored muslin gown sprigged with tiny gold and green leaves. From her neat appearance, one would not guess she'd spent the better part of the day seeing off the guests.

Cate had only a moment in which to plan her strategy. Should she let Isabella know that she knew Isabella knew her secret or should she let Isabella bring it up? Prior experience with difficult fortunes to tell had taught her that when in doubt, the best approach was to let the other lead. She would learn far more about the other party's state of mind if she followed. One only led when one was in a position of power to control the situation. Cate knew that was not the case here. She hadn't the ammunition at her disposal to take the offensive with Isabella. She would let Isabella expose her hand and then she could react appropriately.

"Are they all gone?" Cate asked with a forced air of friendliness.

"Yes." Isabella's tone was distant. "Getting the guests out is almost as difficult as getting them settled."

Isabella leveled her distinctive topaz eyes at Cate. It was all the warning she would get. "Cecile and I have rang for tea to be served in the music room. It's quiet and offers a serene prospect in the late afternoon with its view of the gardens. Will you join us? All the loose ends from the house party are being wrapped up even as we speak. All except one."

The imperious tone of her voice made it clear she was not *asking* Cate to join them. She was commanding it. Only a coward would seek a way out, and Cate was no coward. Attaining Spelthorne would not be accomplished through spineless acts but by unabashedly proclaiming who she was. If she could not face two women, she'd never muster the pluck to face far more dangerous audiences. She reminded herself sternly as she followed Isabella down the warren of hallways leading to the music room that she was in possession of the truth. She was doing nothing wrong by asking for what was legitimately hers.

The music room was indeed a place of potential quietude. The walls were painted a deep summer blue and finished with white wainscoting. An elegant carpet featuring a peacock in blues, greens, and gold lay on the floor. A small fireplace done in white to complement the wainscoting sat on one wall, around which was arranged the conversation area where they sat—Isabella presiding on the curved sofa upholstered in blue damask, Cecile and she perched on matching elegant chairs.

About the room, various instruments were placed: a harp, a pianoforte, and a violin. If the situation were different, Cate would have been eager to get her hands on the violin, which shone from good care and varnishing. If the situation was different, the room would live up to Isabella's claim of serenity. But today, the air was infused with tension.

Isabella poured out the tea from a blue and white china teapot, giving an oral tour of the room as she did so. "This tea set is by the Josiah Spode Company. Giles is an avid collector of all things regal. His table is set with nothing but the best. He has one of the premier collections of Spode and Wedgwood china in the *ton*. He bought this set especially for this room since the color and pattern complement it so well.

"In fact, he had the decorators paint these walls

'Wedgwood blue' on purpose. The furniture is all done in the Louis XV style. In the smaller, more intimate rooms of the abbey, Giles has adopted the Regence fashion for furnishings like he has here. You will note the delicate tracery on the arms and legs of the chairs you and Cecile occupy. The rosewood used for them shows off the workmanship in a most excellent fashion." Isabella broke off her commentary. "Sugar with your tea?"

Cate declined and accepted the splendid cup and saucer from Isabella. She was feeling overwhelmed by the amount of information Isabella had imparted. To her, the walls were simply blue like the summer sky she'd camped beneath her entire life. The exquisite tea set that matched its surroundings so perfectly was only a happy coincidence. She had looked at the room, found it beautiful but nothing more. Giles had looked at this room and seen a place to make a masterpiece where every element was carefully considered and laid out. Nothing was left to chance.

If a bowstring were as taut as the tension filling the room, it would snap. Isabella's lesson could have not been more obviously taught. Cate actually felt an enormous sense of relief when Isabella handed Cecile a teacup and fixed Cate with a stare that indicated it was time to get down to business. "I can see from my recitation, that you have no inkling of what I am talking about and why it is important."

Cate said nothing but merely held Isabella's gaze. The countess might be right, but Cate didn't have to admit defeat.

A hint of a smile danced on Isabella's lips. "Come, Cate. Do you know who Josiah Wedgwood is? Do you know what he did for the improvement of china?"

"No, I do not," Cate said, purposefully keeping her head erect. "Do you know how to read palms? Do you know you can predict a man's future by the length of his life line?"

"Touché," Isabella said, smiling over the rim of her teacup. "I do not. But then, I am not attempting to infiltrate a gypsy camp and lay claim to the position of fortune-teller."

Isabella's tone startled Cate. The last was not said with the biting condemnation she had expected. She also noted Isabella's careful choice of words. Isabella had said "lay claim" when she could have easily have said "pass myself off as." Was there an ally of sorts lurking beneath Isabella's harsh lesson?

Cate decided to test her assumptions. "You mean, *pretending* to be the heir to Spelthorne?"

"No, I mean laying claim," Isabella said sharply. "Whether you and Giles have a legitimate dispute over the claim to Spelthorne is another issue entirely, one which will resolve itself in time. True, Giles is our friend. For me, he's been a friend nearly my whole life. I trailed after him and my brother Alain years before Tristan joined our circle. Last night Cecile and I were shocked to hear the truth behind your sudden appearance at the house party. However, Cecile and I have talked since then and we've come to a conclusion, rather a few conclusions."

Cate sipped her tea to cover her surprise and quirked an eyebrow, practicing one of the gestures she'd seen Isabella make over the course of the last two days. This was growing more interesting by the moment. Either Isabella and Cecile were going to oust her from the house or they had something planned that probably didn't include Giles's seal of approval.

Cecile took over the conversation at this point, giving Cate a chance to study Alain's wife. So much of her interactions with the two ladies had been dominated by Isabella. Now, for the first time, she concentrated on the sherry-eyed woman with lustrous mahogany-colored hair. Cecile was every bit as lovely as Isabella but compared side by side, Cecile lacked the grand presence which Isabella exuded with ease.

In part, this was due to Isabella's striking height, but also Cate recognized it had to do with the breeding of a lifetime. Isabella had been born to be one of society's leading ladies. Cate had seen it in her that very first night on the Denbigh's back verandah when she'd predicted Isabella would become a grande dame of the *ton*.

Cecile's soft, French-accented tones drew Cate's attention almost as much as what the woman was saying. "Bella is right. Perhaps you and Giles have something to work out. Yes, we were at first upset about the challenges you made against our friend. However, those challenges will be resolved and when they are, you will have a new life, no matter what the decision is. You knew very well the risk you took the moment you stepped foot onto Spelthorne. There would be no going back to the caravan no matter what happened here."

"That's not true. The caravan would welcome me back," Cate stammered. The references to a "new life" were confusing.

Cecile smile softly and gave a gentle shake of her head. "*Ma cherie,* I am sure they would. However, I am just as sure that you would never be happy there again as you were in the past. It would never satisfy you. I know. That was how it happened for me. When I met Alain, I knew nothing would ever be the same for me. Through him, I saw that there was another way to live. I simply had to reach out and grasp it. Knowing that, I could not go back to the old way of living."

"Wait." Cate set down her teacup forcefully. "I am not in love with the earl. You talk as if there is romance brewing. There is nothing more between us than a legal matter."

Cecile nodded and gave a Gallic wave of her hand. "I am not talking of love, at least not yet. My love for Alain is an entirely different story, one that I might share at another time for another purpose. I only mean to say that once we meet certain people in our lives, they change those lives irrevocably, romance and love withstanding."

"Just as long as we're clear on that," Cate said sharply, feeling uncomfortable with the discerning glance Isabella cast her direction.

"The point being, you will have a new life. Your new life has already begun. Look at you." Cecile gestured to the dress Cate wore. "You're dressed fashionably, your hair is done up by a lady's maid. You're drinking English tea from a Spode cup. You attended a ball and danced with gentlemen. These are things which will occur routinely in this new life you are embarking on."

Cate stared blankly at Cecile. *What was the woman getting at?*

Isabella broke in. "What Cecile is trying to say in a polite way is that these are ordinary behaviors in your new life and you are ill-equipped to deal with the most mundane of them. If you want to change your life, you must do so entirely. It is not enough to have a fine dress or any of the other outer trappings of a better life. You must change on the inside too. That means you must learn how to get on at a ball, how to pay an afternoon call, how to purchase your own wardrobe, how to lay out menus and organize the staff.

"Giles tells us that he's called for the vicar who can vouch for the identity issue and that it will take a month for him to arrive. That means we have only thirty days, more or less depending on the state of the roads, to teach you what you must know in order to get along."

So that was what the tea was about. For a moment Cate was stunned. She looked down at her hands, not feeling on the defensive for the first time since entering the room. "I don't know what to say. I find your offer overwhelming and truthfully, I find it too generous. Why would you do this for me? I am a stranger at best and a potential enemy at worst, although I don't mean to be."

"It is simple," Cecile said, reaching over to squeeze

Cate's hand in an old gesture of feminine affection. "We are women of an age. Women must always band together, especially when men conspire to know and do what is best for us.

"Tristan and Alain and even Giles most likely only see the issue of legitimacy in this situation. I doubt any of them see beyond it to what happens afterward. Men don't have the foresight women do when it comes to people," Cecile said sagely, giving a light laugh. "My dear husband has built a seaside resort in Hythe. He had the forethought for the economic future of the middle class—one where they'd be able to afford vacations and the time to take them, but he nearly lost me because he, like most men, lacked intuition. Besides, I know from experience how much a woman in a new place needs the counsel of other women with experience. I needed Bella when I first married Alain and now it's my turn to pass on that assistance to you."

Cate glanced at Isabella. "And you? Why would you do this for me?"·

Isabella laughed. "You routed Lady Fox-Haughton as if she were no more than lint on your sleeve. I despise the woman, and I relish any opportunity to see that pompous dragon cut down to size, especially when I can be involved in the cutting." Then Isabella sobered. "While that's the truth, I am not that petty. You thwarted her. In the process, you've acquired a powerful enemy. If you seek to move in circles where you will encounter her, you will need armor. She will exploit any weakness you show her no matter how small. Heaven help you if she discovers she was thwarted by a gypsy queen. If we're successful, she won't suspect that you're anything other than a remote cousin of Giles's."

Cate gave a tremulous smile. "Thank you. When I first came to tea I didn't expect this to happen. I expected to be ambushed. You should know I don't mean any harm to Giles. He's shown me every courtesy and treated me far better than a stranger with ill tidings deserves."

Cate found herself fixed with another of Isabella's stares. She lowered her teacup to meet it.

"My dear Cate, no matter what happens, you will change his life. You already have. It is a great power to shape another's life. For the rest of his, he will remember you in some way. The only choice you have is how you shape that remembrance."

Isabella poured another cup of tea for every one. "We mean you as little harm as you mean Giles," She imparted meaningfully, raising her teacup for a toast. "Here's hoping it stays that way." The three of them clinked their delicate cups gently and sipped.

Cate did not miss the implied meaning beneath Isabella's toast. All in all, Cate thought the act quite civil in comparison to the promised unsheathing of claws that could follow should she harm Giles in any way. She suspected that whatever punishments Lady Fox-Haughton could mete out would pale against the vengeance Isabella could wreak on behalf of a maligned friend.

Chapter Nine

Since her tea with Isabella and Cecile, Cate's days took on a regular and yet daunting routine; mornings were spent with the ladies studying the precedence of the peerage, learning the intricacies of household management, and the arts of carrying off social situations ranging from dinners *enfamille* to the society ball. There were lessons in the meticulous details of each context: seating arrangements, table settings, which fork to use at dinner parties, instruction in popular card games such as Cassino, Speculation, and Commerce along with the mastery of dancing and the delicacies of small talk. There were also lessons in the things Isabella deemed mundane—planning one's wardrobes for the seasons: the Little Season, the Winter Season, summers at the estate and fall hunting parties.

Cate had always lived her life attuned to the seasons: the fall of the leaves in autumn, the bleakness of winter, the rebirth of spring, and the full vibrancy of summer. To Cate, the change of the seasons had rotated on cycles of nature. Now, under Isabella's tutelage, she was introduced to a new rhythm—a rhythm dominated by events instead of buds and tender new shoots.

She learned that the season might start after Easter but wasn't official until the royal art exhibition at the academy, usually held in May. The season ended not with the heat of summer that made London nearly intolerable in July but in August, August 12 to be precise, correlating with the closure of parliament.

Cate recognized in hindsight how her lack of knowledge regarding the intricacies of Giles's life could have been quite damning. If she'd been left on her own, free to find her "own level," she would have foundered immediately. All the rituals and practices that Giles observed were quite foreign to her practical life.

From Cate's perspective and experience, it was difficult to see why it mattered that one attend the Royal Regatta at Brighton or be on hand at Ascot, even if one didn't have a horse racing. Why should one bother with an extensive wardrobe of gowns intended to be worn no more than twice? To a woman who had the privilege of owning two complete outfits each year, the requirements of a true lady's wardrobe seemed outlandish, inefficient, and highly uneconomical.

Isabella was patient and tolerant to a degree. When Cate balked at the extensive lessons laid out before her,

Isabella would straighten her shoulders and fix her protégé with a piercing topaz stare and remind her that the mark of a lady was not the cut of her gown but the depth of her manners. A true lady knew how to carry on in any situation and in the face of any adversity no matter how small or how major. A true lady could be relied upon at all times to do and say just the right thing in the just the right way.

While the lessons were tiring, they were also intriguing. Cate had always had a great fascination for how other people of any social status lived. Part of the charm of traveling with the caravan was a chance to see all of England and all of its various peoples. Learning about the *ton* was no less exciting than learning about the sheep farming communities of the Cotswolds.

But there was time to learn about nature as well as society. Isabella relinquished her claim on Cate's time after luncheon. If Cate could pick a time of day that pleased her most it would be the afternoons, which were alternately spent with Giles touring the estate or at her leisure. For the latter afternoons, she spent her time strolling the grounds of the estate, marveling in the autumnal beauty of Spelthorne's gardens and forests or, when weather did not permit such outdoor activity, in the music room playing on the violin she'd spied the day Isabella had invited her tea.

Those were good days, quiet days when she found a semblance of inner peace in a world that had upended itself. She was honest enough with herself to admit that the carefully dressed and coiffed woman who looked back at her in the looking-glass was far from the brassy woman who had risked all by coming to Spelthorne three weeks ago with her bold claim.

The days she did not spend with her own pursuits, she spent with Giles, receiving an instruction of a different sort. While Isabella and Cecile taught her the art of manners amongst the *ton,* Giles taught her estate management. He gave her free use of an excellent bay mare in his stables, and together they would ride the length and breadth of the estate. She was impressed by the extent of his holdings. There was a home farm which generated the crops that fed the manor, the tenant farmers, and the villagers. There were the village merchants ranging from the butcher, baker, a dressmaker, and other myriad small businesses that contributed to the self-sustaining lifeblood of Spelthorne.

Not only was Giles responsible for the economic survival of Spelthorne through the successful managing of business and agricultural needs, he also oversaw the spiritual needs of his people. The parish vicarage was part of his holding, and it was his job to bestow that living on a worthy individual who could provide ethical guidance to the people of Spelthorne.

She had not guessed, could not have begun to guess, at the profundity of his obligations. She learned that when Giles was not riding the lands talking to cottagers about new roofs for winter, or inquiring about the impact of taxes on local merchants, making rounds to offer the latest agricultural advice on crop rotation to farmers, or visiting shut-in parishioners with the vicar in the afternoons, he spent the mornings in his study poring over ledgers, paying bills, writing correspondence, and attending to issues of parliament which committees had addressed to him during the off-season.

When Cate commented to Isabella that Giles needed a secretary, Isabella retorted that Giles didn't need a secretary so much as he needed a wife. A wife would be able to take up the visits to the tenants, establish groups for the ladies, and keep an ear open to the news of the village, without Giles having to be there personally.

With a wife he would be free to spend more time on parliament issues and agriculture, leaving the spiritual life and interpersonal workings of his holdings to his wife's capabilities. While he would ultimately make decisions on quarter day when the farmers and villagers brought their issues before the earl, those decisions would be significantly influenced by his wife's perspective. Isabella pointed out that the wife would be the one to know what the dowry should be for the butcher's daughter who was betrothed to the miller's son.

Cate found Isabella's not-so-subtle message daunting. If she attained her goal of acquiring Spelthorne, she would be faced with an enormous task. It was apparent from her afternoon rides with Giles that his tenants adored him, trusted him to safeguard their livelihoods. After all, it was Giles who negotiated the market prices for their crops, who decided when new roofs were needed and which roofs would last another year. He decided which crops were planted and which fields lay fallow.

Everyone respected him and because of their respect
for him, they allowed her, a stranger, to move among
them, to learn their ways. She did not doubt that the
people of Spelthorne would be less open to her if she'd
come on her own or if they'd known her true purpose
for being there. One thing was clear to her—no one saw
Giles Moncrief as less than the rightful heir. They were
proud of their earl, proud to work for a man who respected them and knew them.

She knew how they felt for she felt that way too. When
she would look back over her month at Spelthorne in the
later years of her life, she would recall first and foremost
not the lessons Isabella drilled her in, not the substantial
reconfiguration of her life as she slowly transformed
from a Rom who lived outside of society to a lady of
quality, but the man, Giles Moncrief.

If what Isabella said about Cate's ability to influence
Giles's life, the reverse was also true about Cate's ability. Simply knowing him changed her in countless ways.
He taught her innumerable lessons without opening his
mouth. He taught her the true merit of a gentleman. A
gentleman dressed cleanly, immaculately, stylishly,
without putting on the foppish habits of a dandy. A gentleman didn't need bright colors and peacockish affec-
tations. A gentleman maintained his honor always, even
when temptation presented an easier route. A gentleman
could be judged by the behavior he exhibited not only
among his equals but the behavior he displayed in his
treatment of those beneath his social status—those who

looked to him and relied on his guidance for their liveli-hood. Giles was all those things. Chivalrous to a fault.

It was a fault she would not have seen if she had not lived in close proximity with him. The first time she'd en-countered him years ago telling fortunes, she had taken his measure, and correctly so. She had seen him as an up-standing man of honor who wore fine clothes and carried himself well. She had not seen beyond that or had even an inkling of what those abilities required of him.

To her, originally, he'd led a life of ease and luxury, devoid of responsibilities. Now, riding by his side through the harvesting of the crops or standing beside him as he talked with the vicar, she understood fully what it meant to be a Spelthorne. To Giles Moncrief, it was not a way of life, it was his life. He had given his all, the sum of his being, to the running of his estates.

Years ago Cate had admired him from afar for his handsome looks and regal bearing. His golden good looks would do any fairy-tale prince proud from the pages of a child's book. In retrospect, what she'd felt for him was probably nothing more than a type of envy, a covetousness of wanting what was out of reach. The man she knew now was worthy of her true admiration for something beyond his looks and bearing.

As the days grew closer to the arrival of the vicar, Cate found herself faced with three realizations that shook the core of her being and challenged her sensi-bilities. First, she more than admired Giles Moncrief. He had far superseded any of her expectations.

True to his word, he had not kissed her since that first night in his chambers, nor had he given any indication of treating her as less than a lady. He had not used his status as lord of the manor to seduce her or take ungentlemanly advantage of her position.

It was something of a shock for her to recognize that she wished he would. When she'd look at him across the supper table, ride by his side across the fields, or share a friendly smile across the card table in the evening, she would recall with all too vivid recollection the feel of his hands on her body when he'd gathered her in his arms, the press of his lips, the fire of his passion. She wanted to live the passion again, when he had met her as a man and not as the earl.

But he was the earl, first, last, always. That was the second realization and perhaps most damning. He was the embodiment of Spelthorne. He was indisputably the lifeblood of Spelthorne. To deprive this place of him, would be to take away its heart. Long before the vicar arrived, Cate knew she couldn't allow that to happen.

The third realization frightened her. All that Magda had predicted since the night of the ball had come to pass. Magda had warned her against the folly of falling for the earl, of allowing herself to play at the fairy tale she'd whole-heartedly concocted for herself.

Magda had warned her about being able to separate myth from reality when the time came. The time was swiftly approaching and Cate knew she was ill-prepared to deal with the situation of her making. She had set her destiny in motion and now, for the sake of a man who did not guess the depth of her feeling for him or who did guess and did not reciprocate those feelings, she was willing to throw her future away. Practicality told her her choice was ludicrous but intuition told her something else was afoot at Spelthorne, as the month of October headed into its final week.

Cate did not doubt the strength of her intuition; it was what made her such a success as a fortune-teller, sham though she was. She'd never had the "sight" the way some of the other tellers did. But she had her own sight. She could see people and their penchants from the way they dressed to the way they behaved and treated others.

It was her sight that bothered her most about the month she spent at Spelthorne, surrounded by people who meant her well but, as she was coming to realize with disappointing clarity, did not believe her claims would come to fruition.

Isabella and Cecile were teaching her deportment. Giles was showing her the running of the estate. Neither of them were showing her because they thought she would be taking over the reins at Spelthorne. Nor were they imparting their knowledge in an elaborate scheme to make her recognize her inferiority and decamp as Magda believed. They had something else, something secret, planned for her.

The "secret plan conspiracy" which she privately labeled her unease, grew in merit as she contemplated the interactions over the past weeks. Isabella and Cecile had made several references about "her new life" using the phrase "regardless of what is decided here." Cecile had talked at length about the inability to "go back" to her old life.

As October waned, Cate began to get the sense that a surprise of sorts was being planned. The caravan had once planned a secret party for Tommasino to celebrate his birthday. For two weeks, they'd all crept about, carrying out their mysterious little tasks to acquire a gift, decorations, and the ingredients to bake a cake. It had been fun, even exciting then, but she'd been on the other side of things. She decided being the recipient of a surprise wasn't nearly as wonderful as planning the surprise.

Thus, her last week was not filled with the things she wanted to remember most about Spelthorne. Instead of enjoying the scarlet leaves and the honking of geese as they winged over the lake heading south, she was plagued with anxiety on two fronts. She was trying to unravel the mystery of what her new life might be in the eyes of the others, and she was trying desperately to find a solution to the situation with Giles.

She loved him. Unrequited or not, her feelings for him would not allow her to be the instrument of his undoing. She did not want to hear the vicar pronounce her story as true. It would break Giles, and she could not face a world without his goodness in it. People needed a man like him to follow. No, she would not let him falter. But neither could she turn her back on what was rightfully hers.

"What am I to do, Magda," she said one night, flopping down on the fluffy blue counterpane in distress. "If I uphold the truth of my story, he is dethroned and I cannot live with myself for causing that. If I deny my story, he will be justified in evicting me and in every negative thought he ever had about me. I will have lived up to any stereotype concocted about the Rom and I will have lived up to any bad impression he may have formed. I will be admitting that I am a fraud, a liar, a cheat, willing to whore myself. I will, as Isabella is fond of saying, "have found my own level." As a man of honor, Giles will have nothing to do with me at that point. That option, too, is unpalatable to me."

Cate watched Magda pace several lengths of the bedroom, tapping her finger thoughtfully against her chin. "Answer me this," she said when she spoke at last. "Is it Spelthorne you covet or the man?"

Cate spoke slowly, watching Magda carefully. "Although you warned me against him, it is the man I've come to covet, not the estate."

"Perhaps there is a way to still have both but it will mean a little pain in the short term. You must uphold your claim, not because you mean to unseat him. You must uphold it and use it as the leverage to coax a marriage proposal from him."

Cate sat upright on the bed. "Marriage! But he doesn't love me."

"Loving you is irrelevant although I'd wager he is not as indifferent to you as you think. What he does love is without a doubt is Spelthorne. Marriage is the perfect solution to your dilemma. You can keep the man, and he can keep his precious estate. Who knows, perhaps that is what the ladies have been planning all along," Magda said mystically.

Chapter Ten

Magda's suggestion that Giles was not as indifferent to her as she might have believed cast his interactions with her the next day in a new light, which was not necessarily to his advantage. His behavior was as correct as always as he gave her a leg up onto her mare. As a neutral gentleman or even as a friend, the action was quite proper. As a potential suitor who may want to let a woman know he was interested in her, the action was quite lacking. It was surely possible that Magda was just wrong in her assumptions. But Magda seldom erred where men and women were concerned.

The extreme correctness in his manner and conversation as they rode seemed more pronounced than usual and Cate was struck with the urge to ruffle his demeanor, to see him flummoxed the way she found herself oft times bestirred in his presence. If Magda had not suggested such feeling might exist beneath the surface, Cate would not have guessed it was there. This afternoon she felt compelled not only to ruffle his calm exterior but to test the presence of his feelings. If Magda was right, Cate wanted to know before the vicar arrived, which would surely be any day.

"It's a lovely day for this late into autumn," Cate said, bringing her horse alongside his big roan hunter. Isabella had taught her weeks ago that for some inexplicable reason the English were obsessed with conversation over the weather. It seemed a good time to try out that particular conversational gambit.

Indeed, she had not exaggerated her claim. The sun shone bright in a clear sky. The fall foliage overhead as they passed beneath the trees of Spelthorne Wood was brilliant in hues of scarlet and gold. The sharpness of the afternoon air served as a reminder that while the day was a treasure, summer was truly behind them and winter loomed ahead. Once beneath the trees, the misleading patches of warmth in which they had ridden from the house vanished, giving way to a coolness that made Cate thankful for the warmth of her riding cloak.

"It may be one of the last great days we see for months," Giles agreed. "Alain and Tristan left this morning to do some grouse hunting. They should have had a good day for shooting."

"Is that the River Ash?" Cate gestured to a glimmering ribbon in the distance.

"Yes, it forms the north boundary of Spelthorne."

"It doesn't look far. Shall we ride toward it? I would like to see it."

Giles nodded his assent and took the lead as the bridle path narrowed, deftly wending his way through the forest and out into the sunlight again. A meadow lay between the woods and the river, allowing them a good gallop after the placid walk beneath the trees.

At the river, Cate waited to let Giles help her dismount, giving him a chance to take a quiet liberty or two by leaving his hands at her waist longer than necessary but he did not. Instead, he properly offered her his arm so that she could steady herself on the uneven ground leading down to the river. Impishly, Cate refused. For all the manners she'd acquired in the last month, she loved the out of doors and had grown up having to fend for herself. With one hand, she grabbed up the skirt of her habit, lifting high enough above the tops of her boots so that she would not trip, and made her way down to the edge of the shore.

The silvery ribbon she'd seen at a distance was browner close up, an earthy river that ran over agates. She could see large fish swimming in the shadows of the shallows. Cate shielded her eyes and looked down the river into the distance. "When I see a river, I always wonder where it goes, what it sees."

Beside her, Giles skipped stones into the current. "This river sees farms and small towns. It passes through Ashford and Shepperton before it joins with the Thames in Sunbury."

"Ah," Cate sighed whimsically. "A farmer's river that goes to town, goes to London."

"A farmer's river? I suppose it is. I've never thought of it that way before."

Cate turned to look at Giles in profile as he tossed the stones, one booted leg raised and resting on a large boulder. He flicked his wrist and sent another one sailing into the stream. It bounced four times. "Hah! Four! That's the best I've done today." He crowed triumphantly, a brilliant smile wreathing his face.

The act caused Cate's breath to catch. The action was so full of life, so animated that she realized she was seeing Giles with the bridle of his manners—seeing *him* although it was no more than a glimpse really of a man who enjoyed sport, the outdoors, competition and quite simply being. Throughout the entire month at Spelthorne, she'd constantly seen the earl in him. She had not once been able to see the earthy cottager's son. She saw a piece of him now and found him entrancing, if not more so than the earl. An idea took shape in her head.

She studied the fish. "Unless I miss my guess, those are trout."

"Yes," Giles said in surprise. "You know fish?"

She tossed her head and laughed up at him with a smile. "Most definitely. In the summer and spring, the caravan relied on fish for its meat source. We all fished or we didn't eat. Those trout there look like two of them would provide a tasty meal."

Giles chuckled. "I know from first hand experience that they do. As soon as I turned eight and could run amok in the summers, I spent many hours and many lunches down here. There's a better fishing hole further upstream."

Cate walked to a nearby tree hanging over the river and tested a willowy bough. Finding it to her liking, she broke it neatly off and waved the new switch through the air. "I breakfasted late this morning and was not hungry enough to eat again when luncheon was served," she said, her invitation and intention clear underscored in her message.

"You are not suggesting we fish?" Giles asked, the mask of the earl sliding over the visage of the exultant cottager's son.

She nodded. "I am suggesting precisely that. Are you game?"

"We haven't got fishing line or bait." He argued.

"Then we'll improvise." Cate smiled wickedly and lifted her riding habit to reveal the starched whiteness of a petticoat. With a deft move she ripped a length of it before rucking up her skirts and briefly showing off a small leather sheathe strapped to her leg. She whipped out a sharp dagger and laughed at the shock Giles tried to hide.

She proceeded to strap the dagger to the willow switch with the length of fabric. "There. I am ready. How are you coming with your equipment?"

"You can't be serious. It is unseemly."

"How unseemly can it be? It's just us. No one will know," Cate cajoled. "It will be fun."

"Fun? That's something I haven't had in a very long time," Giles said, indecision warring with propriety.

"Alright. I'm in." Giles shrugged out of his coat and pulled off his meticulously tied cravat. Then, to Cate's delight, he sat on the boulder, tugged off his boots and bared his feet, shoving his trousers up to his knees.

The sight of a bare-legged Giles sans coat, standing before her in nothing but skin-tight buff riding breeches and thin linen shirt was intoxicating. Watching him wade into the river with his makeshift fishing spear courtesy of his cravat and hunting knife was positively striking.

Cate knotted her skirts and stripped off her shoes and waded in after him. "Brrr! This water is cold!" She cried at first contact. "I'd forgotten it wasn't summer."

Giles looked up from his quarry. "You won't catch cold will you? Perhaps you should wait on shore."

Cate grinned. "And let you have all the fun when it was my idea in the first place? Besides, I'm Rom. If we got sick every time we waded in cold rivers, we'd never be well." The thought was out before she realized what she was saying. No one at Spelthorne talked about her gypsy life. No one asked about her past. It was understood to be taboo. "I'm sorry. I shouldn't have said that," she said to cover the awkward moment.

"Why would you be sorry?"

"Because I'm not supposed to talk about it."

"Did Bella tell you that?" Giles asked in all seriousness.

"No, I just assumed, since no one asked." Cate shrugged and turned her attention back to the fish. "I bet I can spear mine before you get yours," she wagered, hoping to return levity to their adventure.

She succeeded and five long minutes later, Giles won, brandishing his trout with boyish enthusiasm.

Cate put her hands on her hips. "Do you want to know what your prize is?" She said saucily. "You get to start the fire."

While she finished catching her trout, Giles gathered up an armload of twigs and fallen branches and started an admirable fire. Gallantly, he offered to prepare the fish and roast them over a makeshift spit.

Cate leaned back on the old blanket he produced from his saddlebags and spread on the ground, studying him as he worked, the heat of the fire warming her cold toes. "Your saddlebags are conveniently well-stocked," she commented.

"The head groom who taught me to ride when I was growing up also taught me to always ride prepared. I learned to never leave for a trail ride without a tinder box, hunting knife, and a blanket. Three items is not so much to carry and can provide all kinds of comforts if needed." Giles leaned forward and turned the spit. "I think the fish are done." He took down the spit and handed one of the fish to Cate.

"It smells delicious." She took a bite and sighed. "Tastes good too. Food tastes better out of doors, I think." Juices dribbled down her chin, and she futilely tried to lick them.

"I'm sorry I don't have a fork or even a napkin to offer you," Giles apologized. "If this were a real picnic, there would be a table with a cloth, goblets, wine, eating utensils."

Cate laughed at the ridiculous picture his idea of picnic conjured up in her head. "How could that be a real picnic? *This* is a real picnic, us sitting by a fire we made, eating food we caught ourselves. Our clothes are damp and for once we are not thinking about manners and propriety and what everyone else expects." She licked the last of the fish from her hands and turned to face Giles, pulling her knees up under her skirts. "Do you know this is the first time we've talked?"

"That's not true. We've talked numerous times. We talk when we make the rounds in the village. We talk over supper. We talk over cards," Giles protested.

"I mean truly talk about ourselves. That other talk is business, small talk with others present. Today you told me a story about your boyhood. I would like to hear more about the boy Giles." She smiled softly, resting her chin on her knees. "I would like to hear more about the man I saw fishing in the river today. I think that man is vastly more interesting than the earl he devotes all his time to being." The last came out in a rush. She had not meant to push or pry.

Giles rewarded her with a smile and a stretch. He rolled onto his side facing her and propped his head on his hand. "My childhood is unremarkable really, until I met Alain and Chatham. Before that, I was a typical child of nobility, alone and raised by the servants, some of which were doting and some of which were severely strict. My father wasn't here often, and my mother had her obligations which kept her busy making the rounds."

"Like you do," Cate interjected. "Your days are filled with the pursuit of obligations."

"I suppose it is. It is what an earl does," Giles said, slightly defensive.

"It's not all an earl can do," she countered.

"It's what I have chosen to do."

"To the detriment of discovering personal enjoyment," she said sharply and regretting it.

"Not all of us are born to adventure, Cate, like you."

That gave her pause. "Is that how you see me?"

Giles toyed with the fire, poking at the dying embers with a stick. "You have a passion for living that is different than mine. I need order, structure, security. You need none of those things. You are . . . ," here he paused, searching for the word, staring hard at her in a way that made Cate feel warm down to her cold riverwashed toes.

"You are like our river, going wherever the riverbed leads. You're afraid of nothing, you embrace everything. Nothing overwhelms you. You don't seek to conquer or bind. You just seek to be. I could never be like that. It's far too frightening for me to take those risks. I knew the moment I saw you in the garden two years ago that you were so beyond me. I could barely comprehend all that you were. It's more than your beauty, although your's transcends anything I've ever beheld. It's your soul, Cate."

He reached her hand and took it in his own, tracing the lines of her palm with slow strokes. He brought the open palm to his lips and kissed it deeply before pressing it to his cheek. "My divine Cate, I hope we have not done you a disservice with all of our lessons. I would never want to tame you. I find myself liking the woman who fishes in the river and rides in unorthodox races quite a lot."

Cate whispered, "I find I like the man who fishes in the river quite a lot too." She breathed deeply. It was divine having him all to herself, without the presence of his well-meaning friends. He smelled of earth and water, fish and wood smoke. He smelled even better than he did in the evenings when he came to dinner fresh from his bath, smelling of spice and sandalwood.

She could have sat with him, her hand in his, all afternoon. But the world was calling Giles Moncrief and the moment was over too soon.

"It's starting to get late. We need to get back. The others will worry," he said, rising from the blanket and offering her a hand up. He immured himself in the chore of cleaning up camp, kicking dirt on the fire.

In silence they donned their discarded stockings and shoes. Cate did her best to smooth her wrinkled skirts, but in truth, she didn't want to repair her appearance too much. She wanted Giles to be reminded of what they had enjoyed. When he allowed it, there was a real connection between them, a connection that was not about who was Spelthorne or who had the right to the title.

With gentlemanly precision he helped her mount, and they rode back through the meadow and the woods to the abbey in a disappointing silence. Giles left her at the stables with nothing more than a polite farewell, "Thank you for an entertaining afternoon, I will see you at dinner."

Cate returned to her rooms, determined to spend the short hours before dinner in isolation and contemplation. She rang for a hot bath to warm herself after the coldness of the fishing expedition and the brisk ride home in damp skirts she was careful to hide from prying eyes.

She took an unusually long time dressing for dinner that night. She wanted Giles to see her in all the beauty he confessed her to have. *What kind of woman would Giles want to see at the dinner table?* She pulled out the ice-blue gown with its eau de nil bodice and gauzy flowing skirts. It was one of her favorites since Isabella had helped her to order her own wardrobe. She held the gown against her body and studied it in the mirror.

She discarded it. No. The gown was too sophisticated for the night. Giles would want to see the lady she was in that gown—a woman well cultured and groomed not given to earthy passions or jumping into rivers on a whim. She pulled out several others and discarded them as well for being too tame, too ladylike, too molded. She needed something bolder, more daring yet confident. She reached into the back of the wardrobe and found what she was looking for. The gown was not modern but it was the kind of gown she'd dreamed of owning for years. She had described it to the modiste who'd come to the abbey and done her other dresses. The modiste had clapped her hands in delight at the thought of creating something extraordinary and had shown her a bolt of shimmering rose-red silk. Cate had fingered the bolt longingly. The red was perfect. It was not a scarlet, nor a harlot's red. It was a regal, royal red.

Cate called a maid other than Magda, not wanting to brook any censure over her choice of gown. Now that her mind was made up, she would not be swayed from her course.

The maid helped her lace up the necessary corset and put on the layers of petticoats required for the long, tight bodice and full skirts. Then she slipped the rich gown over her head, fastening it up the back and helping Cate to tug the v-ed waist of the bodice into place and to fluff the layers of silken skirts to best effect. The gown left her neck and shoulders exposed and Cate fastened a string of borrowed pearls about her neck before sitting down to let the maid arrange her hair in a complicated upsweep that left the back of her neck exposed with the exception of a few loose curls. The final result was all that Cate had hoped for. She hoped Giles would get the message.

Giles arrived in the drawing room at promptly 6:30, the standard half hour before dinner was served, dressed for the evening and dismayed to learn that while he'd been out riding with Cate, Isabella and Cecile had decided to turn the evening into a party of sorts. It was no less than what he deserved for gallivanting about the countryside, fishing in his bare feet, in October no less.

Isabella and Cecile were already there ahead of him, dressed in gowns that were definitely too elegant for an *enfamille* supper in the country. He smiled harmlessly at the women and joined them. "To what do I owe the pleasure of your impromptu party plans?"

"Don't be mad, Giles," Isabella began. "It's the end

of the month, and I just thought we all deserved a little celebrating."

The end of the month—quite possibly the last quiet night before the vicar arrived and the tension which they had all successfully held at bay for four weeks would break loose. Although Giles was confident all would end well—he had found a lovely old manor of moderate size for Cate to lease in Hertfordshire—feelings were bound to be hurt in the short term and it would be difficult for all of them.

He nodded his approval and turned to greet Tristan and Alain who entered together, freshly washed from their hunting expedition. The twosome regaled the group with their exploits, filled which much teasing over who actually had bagged the better grouse. Giles couldn't help but think of his own expedition to the river. The thought was quite distracting, but not nearly so distracting as the vision gracing the door way. It took a moment to register that the woman was Cate.

His manners faltered. The old-styled gown from the previous century hugged her slender waist to perfection, the puffed sleeves that started just below her shoulder showed her creamy skin to advantage. The full skirts swayed and shushed sensually as she moved toward the group. The upsweep of her hair lent her a regal air. Not for the first time, Giles thought, "Snow White." A Snow White for adults. Then he thought, that was precisely what she wanted him to think, what had inspired the daring gown. Snow White, the story of a princess hidden away in the servants' quarters, dressed in the rags of a slave. But nothing could dim the true goodness of her heart. What was the moral his old nurse had told him? That a princess is more than beauty? That was it, a princess was a princess because of what was in her heart. He had said as much to Cate at the river that afternoon. He was certain she was reminding him of that with her choice of gown.

Of course, being a boy, he'd scoffed at his nurse's moral, saying he wasn't interested in the tales of princesses. They were for girls. His nurse had reminded him that the story was about a prince too. That prince was smart enough, good enough in his own heart to see the purity and goodness of others beyond their clothes and fancy manners. The prince had loved her when she was a serving girl long before he awakened her with love's first kiss.

That part made him shift uncomfortably. Cate and he had awakened much more down at the river and his body would be a long time forgetting it.

The butler thankfully announced supper and they traipsed in, ready to enjoy the meal. True to their word, Cecile and Isabella made the occasion festive with candlelight on the table and the laying out of the abbey's finest china. The look on Cate's face when she saw the table laid out in all its splendor was priceless and filled Giles with satisfaction at being the one who could provide her which such a slice of luxury. How many nights had he eaten on this same china with guests who had not once acted the least impressed or appreciative of the beauty laid before them? Cate's appreciation was refreshing.

Despite his earlier apprehension, the meal was a relaxing, enjoyable affair. Wine and conversation flowed easily between the six of them and laughter reigned. After dessert they all adjourned to the music room where Isabella had ordered a fire laid and lamps lit so that there could be music. Cecile was an accomplished violinist, and she entertained them until Isabella persuaded Cate to join Cecile.

Cecile always traveled with her own violin and the spare violin could not be denied. Giles added his own voice to Isabella's. "I would love to hear you play. Isabella says you play wondrously, but I am away from the house apparently when you practice."

Cate rose and smoothed her skirts. She hesitantly picked up the violin and fiddled with the strings. Cecile set out a sheaf of music. "I'll start, jump in when you're ready."

The music Cecile had selected was the music of the English countryside, simple love songs and ballads. Giles thought it was the finest he'd heard. Cate was an excellent musician, her music full of heart and feeling. After a while, he noted Cecile stepped back and put down her violin. Cate was too far gone to notice she was playing alone. Her eyes were shut as she swayed with the violin, her fingers flying over the strings. In her full skirts, her movements were hypnotic. She was playing gypsy music now, Giles was sure of it. The notes of the violin evoked images of bonfires and dancers swaying to an earthy rhythm. He could have listened to her play for hours, and he might have had not a discreet scratch on the door drawn his attention.

Reluctantly he rose to answer it in hushed tones. "Reginald, what is it?" he whispered, not wanting to disturb the performance.

"A note, my lord. It came for you just now." Reginald held out the silver salver, revealing the sealed white stationery.

Dread filled Giles. "Thank you, Reginald. You may retire."

Before turning back to the group, he cracked the seal and read the brief missive. It was as he suspected. He felt someone beside him. It was Alain.

"What is it?" Alain asked, not bothering to whisper. The music had stopped, and everyone was looking expectantly in his direction.

Giles swallowed and mastered his emotions. He scanned the room, wanting to remember the way they all looked on their last evening. He wanted to remember Cate, regal and beautiful in her red gown, her face soft in the lamplight before all hell broke loose. Before he had to send her away.

"It's a note from the inn. The vicar has arrived. He will be here at the abbey tomorrow morning. We are to expect him at ten o'clock."

Chapter Eleven

Morning arrived early and passed slowly. Giles tried to act as if nothing out of the ordinary was occurring with the vicar's impending visit. He rose at 6:00 after spending a sleepless night in his chambers, not daring to go down to the study lest one of the servants become curious about the late night lights. He dressed for his usual morning ride and set out alone.

The ritual of the morning ride offered him a chance to organize his thoughts for the day, lay out his plans. This morning was no different in that respect, only his thoughts were. Tristan and Alain had quietly assured him last night that all would be well. He knew they had worked diligently the past month on his behalf to establish his identity should it become necessary. It would take an army of legal experts to get past Tristan and Alain. Aside from legitimate avenues of proof, Giles also knew he had the issue of status and credibility on his side. There were favors that could be called in, favors that could be bestowed in order to set the record in his favor. He didn't want to win that way. But if it came to that, if that was the only way to keep Spelthorne, would he do it? In spite of his claims to Cate that having ethics meant not applying them haphazardly when one felt like it, Giles was not at all sure what he might feel compelled to do to keep Spelthorne. That troubled him greatly. He did not like to think there was such a weak spot in his armor. He hoped he wouldn't have to find out.

Giles spurred his big hunter forward as he approached a grassy flat area, preparing to give the horse his head. The rush of cold morning wind ruffled his bare head and the crisp air in his face served to exorcise at least briefly the quandary over what he might be driven to do.

He reined in the horse at the top of the rise on the other side of the grassy area. He had not deliberately chosen to come this way but now that he had, new thoughts assailed him, new doubts. The village lay before him, rosy and peaceful in the early light of a new day. The baker was already plying his trade and the earliest of farmers were arriving with fresh produce and milk. From a distance it was a bucolic sight, hiding the hard work and effort of living these lives every day. Had he really been born to be one of them? What if Cate's information was correct and he was nothing more than a cottager's son? What if he was born to be a common tradesman? For a cottager's son, becoming a tradesman would have been high marks indeed. Most likely, he'd been born to a farming family and not a very successful one at that.

These were the thoughts that had plagued him throughout the night. Giles reached beneath his riding coat and drew out the gold pocket watch he carried. He flipped over the cover. Seven o'clock. Three hours until the verdict. He stared at the timepiece, seeing its elegance as if for the first time. Slowly, he pulled off his riding gloves and deliberately fingered the fine wool fabric of his coat. The three hundred pounds he spent on his wardrobe annually did not seem exorbitant to him against the sparkling backdrop of the *ton* where women of rank spent five hundred pounds a year on a collection of elaborate gowns worn two or three times a piece. However, against the backdrop of village life, three hundred pounds was a fortune. Many of the workers were exceedingly lucky to make ten or fifteen pounds a year.

What if he wasn't Spelthorne? Where would he go? What would he do? He had a college education from Oxford. He supposed he could try his hand at teaching or tutoring. That caused him to shudder. He thought of the severely dressed tutors that had traipsed through his life in their serviceable, worn black coats and trousers. He shuddered as much from the possibility as he did from the realization that he feared poverty. He was something of a spoilt young man, fearful of living without the easy luxuries he'd been surrounded by.

Perhaps Cate would let him keep a few things. What

would she let him keep? What should he ask for? His horse? An annual allowance? Maybe she would consider pensioning him off. He grimaced at that. He didn't like the idea of living under the strictures of another person's allowance. He would feel kept, owned. Dependent on another. It didn't take long to see that that was precisely what he'd planned for her fate. He liked to think that situation was different. The manor in Shepperton would be a step up for her, a large step. Still, she would be reliant on him for any increase or permission for an extra purchase. No, he wouldn't like it any more than he was starting to expect she would, no matter that his motives had been good ones. Still, he would offer—if it was his to offer.

These were maudlin thoughts! He had to shake them. He wheeled the big hunter around and set him off at a blister pace, giving himself over to the thrill of ride, deliberately seeking hedges to jump, creeks to gallop through until at last Spelthorne Abbey came into view and he cantered his steaming steed into the stable yard, calling for a groom as if he were lord of the manor and nothing was about to change that. Of course, nothing was. He had let his imagination run away with him out there in the meadows. Spelthorne was his. He had no reason to believe Cate had any claim to it, that the story in the journal was real.

Everyone except Cate was assembled in the breakfast parlor when he strode in. He tried not to notice the awkward silence that fell when he entered the room. Casually, he helped himself to the dishes on the sideboard.

Even though he'd bolstered his confidence in the stable yard, he was struggling to maintain it. The blue and yellow dishes holding the eggs and kippers on the sideboard had been specially made for his mother in Italy. They fit the cheeriness of the room ideally. The silver pots holding the morning chocolate Isabella was so fond off had been done as a wedding gift for his grandparents.

His eyes burned. His throat clogged. Straightening his shoulders, he set his plate down and cleared his throat. "Excuse me. I'd forgotten I have something to do in the study."

In the study, he sank down in one of the leather chairs and stared out the window. There was nothing for it. Between now and 10:00 when the vicar arrived, he was a hopeless sapskull. He couldn't pull his thoughts out of their dark depths.

He wasn't allowed to stew alone for very long. Within ten minutes, Alain and Tristan slipped inside the room and took up their positions—Tristan at the window, hands clasped behind his back, Alain in the chair opposite Giles.

"Are you going to be alright?" Alain asked.

"Ask me in a few hours. I cannot answer that question from where I sit at present," Giles said.

"Do you fear she is right? Is there something you haven't told us?" Tristan asked from the window.

"I've told you all I know." Giles sighed heavily. "There will be no good outcome today. If her claims prove false, she will be devastated. My victory will hurt her. For whatever reason, she believes unerringly in the truth of her claims. She is not a knowing fraud in this. Of course, I've made provisions for her. There is no question of her going back to the gypsy caravan. I've found a house for her in Shepperton. She'll have a solid allowance for the maintenance of her new lifestyle."

Tristan whistled. "That's quite generous of you since she is the one who has come to see you dethroned. I do not know if I would be so forgiving of someone who did as much to me."

"I will not see her hurt."

"Why is that?" Tristan asked, spearing Giles with a dark gaze.

Giles met his friend's inquiry evenly. "I have grown attached to her. She is not evil. She does not do this out of a sense of revenge."

"Do you think she will do the same for you?" Tristan cocked a dark eyebrow.

"I hope it will not come to that. I have tried not to ponder it."

"Unsuccessfully, I am guessing," Alain put in softly.

Giles turned to Alain, unable to bear the burden of his fears alone any longer. "I think a dying man must feel this way when he suspects the end is near. Everything becomes more cherished, more valuable. I wonder what Cate might be convinced to let me keep should I be the one who is in the wrong. But I find I cannot make distinctions between what I would take or leave. All of Spelthorne is wound up together in my history like a big ball of yarn. This morning, I saw my grandparent's silver, my mother's dishes from Italy. Everywhere I look, there is my history, my tradition, at least what I had been taught was my tradition. Spelthorne is me, and I am Spelthorne. I do not know how I could leave it."

"You won't have to," Alain encouraged.

"Alain's right, you know," Tristan argued from the window. "You've put too much weight on the vicar's visit. In reality, this visit only decides what we do next. The vicar is not a court of law. He is merely a witness and mayhap not even a reliable one."

"I suppose your idea of reliable is whether or not he agrees with us?" Giles asked.

"Absolutely. We have options. We just need to select the right options based on our circumstances," Tristan said staunchly.

No one said anything else, but Giles found himself comforted by Tristan's words. The vicar was only the next of many steps in unraveling the mystery Cate had laid before them. He wasn't going to lose Spelthorne, at least not today, and for the present, that seemed to be enough.

The vicar arrived promptly at 10:00 and met by them all in the formal drawing room. Giles had changed out of his riding clothes into proper morning attire. It would have passed as ordinary in London, but for the country, the Spanish blue morning coat with waistcoat, buff inexpressibles, polished Hoby's, and the cravat tied in a "mail coach" knot bespoke of sartorially well-turned out gentleman.

Giles wanted it that way. He did not remember the vicar well since the man had received the offer up north during Giles's youth. Likewise, the vicar did not know him beyond any recollection he might have of a lad at the manor. Giles wanted to make a solid first impression, one that indicated the kind of man he was, the kind of man who ran Spelthorne. He was pleased to note that Alain and Tristan had also taken time to turn themselves out to best advantage. The three of them looked like gentlemen to take seriously. The women were turned out well too in their morning gowns of jaconet muslin.

The picture the five of them presented was formidable, if the vicar's face was any indicator. The vicar was a tall, thin man with a beaky nose and kind eyes. Fading brown hair edging toward sparseness was evident when he removed his hat and handed it to the butler.

Giles came forward. "I am Spelthorne. I am pleased you could undertake the journey and meet with us. I felt that our conversation should take place in person instead of a series of letters for the sake of clarity and resolution. I trust your journey was pleasant? The weather has held remarkably well for fall. The inn is highly recommended, and I've told the innkeeper to send your bill straight to me."

"Thank you," the man said nervously, glancing around the elegant gold and cream drawing room. "Spelthorne is much as I remember it years ago under the previous earl and yet, it seems somehow changed for the better. I am Vicar Robert Waring. It has been years. Twenty two of them since I was a young man here, early in my calling to the church."

"I hope during your stay, you'll make free of the grounds and reacquaint yourself." Giles gestured to a chair between Alain and Tristan's. "Tea shall be served shortly, and then we can begin to unravel the situation. I shall send for Cate. It is time for her to be down here as well since this concerns her."

"There's no need, I'm right here." Cate entered the room before Giles could send off a footman. To her credit she looked nervous, and Giles was struck with a pang of selfishness. While he'd been languishing in the study, he'd had the comfort of his friends' presence. She'd had no one. Surely, she was as nervous about the vicar's visit as he was. Both their lives seemed to hang in the balance of the man's words, of his remembrances. She didn't know, as he did, that the ending was a happy one for her either way. At worst, she'd walk out of here today with the lease on a nice property and an allowance for life.

Once tea was poured out, Giles turned to Robert Waring. "Cate has in her possession two documents that are at the source of our conundrum." This was her cue and she took it, producing the birth certificate and the diary.

"The birth certificate is of main interest to you, Vicar," Giles went on, "since it bears your signature as witness to the birth of a Catherine Celeste Moncrief on the seventeenth day of September." Inwardly he marveled at how calm he sounded. After the emotional strain of the morning, he hadn't been sure he would be up to conducting the interview with his usual savoir faire. Across from him, Cate was pale, her green eyes looking larger than usual against the whiteness of her face.

"The diary is of less importance although it is the source that suggests the baby girl was switched at birth for a boy born the same day." Gingerly Giles handed over the worn red diary, opening it to the entry regarding the events of the fateful night.

The group sat in silence, giving the vicar time to assess the documents and gather his thoughts. "What is that you want to know from me?

Giles cleared his throat. "I want to know if it is true. Did the countess bear a daughter but never a son?"

The vicar looked from Giles to Cate. "I would encourage you both to realize that what I am about to disclose to you does not necessarily affirm anything. It only affirms what I know, which may only be a part of the puzzle. Hypothetically, if I say there was a daughter, it does not prove that this woman here," he gestured to Cate, "is that daughter."

He drew a deep breath and began. "What I know to have happened agrees with the entry in the diary. In order to procure a birth certificate, I had to be shown the baby. Since the labor was not going well, I had been called to the abbey to be on hand should the worst happen. I saw the child as soon as it was born. It was indeed a girl. I did not suspect anything was afoot. I was given my transfer up to York shortly after the child's birth when Spelthorne returned home. I knew nothing of this duplicity until your letter arrived. You must believe I would not have kept quiet about such goings on. But yes, the countess bore a daughter."

He sighed and peered at them all. "I can see that you expected more from me but that is all I know. I signed a birth certificate for Catherine Moncrief. Was this baby switched for a male child? I don't know. Was the countess capable of that? I can only speculate. She was lonely, desperately in love with a husband who did not pay attention to her. I did not know her well enough to make judgments about her."

The vicar picked up the birth certificate again and held it to the light of a window. "There it is. My watermark. I can tell you the certificate is not a forgery. See here, the watermark seal? It was on all of my official documents for the accuracy of record keeping.

"Is the doctor still alive?" he asked.

"No," Giles responded tersely. The long-awaited vicar had not really helped resolve the situation. His information was at once sparse and yet highly informative.

"Too bad. The doctor would perhaps know something of use, a clear clue like a birthmark or a family resemblance," The vicar mused. "My lord, you have golden hair like your father. Miss, you have the dark look of the countess. She had the blackest hair I'd ever seen. But of course, many people in this world bear those traits."

"But no one has this," a stern voice from doorway called.

Everyone turned to see the woman they knew as Cate's maid standing there, from her hand dangled a heavy emerald pendant.

Voices erupted at once.

"You. You're the woman who was at the birth!" exclaimed Waring.

"The Spelthorne emerald!" Giles cried in disbelief. "Where did you get it? It was recorded missing ages ago."

"Magda!" Cate's voice rose above the rest.

Giles's head whipped in her direction. "Magda?" How had they overlooked that? The gypsy healer was here, had been here in this house for weeks. "Why didn't you tell me?" Anger tinged his voice. He felt betrayed.

"Where did you get that?" Tristan said, providing the voice of reason.

Magda strode toward them. "The night the countess gave the child into my keeping, she gave me this as well, to keep safe as part of her birthright. For years I have kept the secret and discharged my duty." She whirled on Giles. "Now it is time to do your duty and step down."

Tristan cut in sharply and seized the necklace. "This may be a fake. If it hasn't been seen for years, how do we know this is the one? No one living would be likely to recognize it," he challenged. "Are there any papers regarding the authenticity of the gem?" he asked Giles.

Giles drew a deep breath. "I believe they are in the safe in the study where all papers of authenticity are kept for the Spelthorne heirlooms. But it will not be necessary." He reached out a hand to steady himself on the arm of the chair. "It was my father's wedding gift to her. It was customary to give it to each countess as a day-after gift. That necklace is in the portrait of my mother hanging in the gallery. She was painted wearing it shortly after their marriage."

Chapter Twelve

Giles paced the gallery later that afternoon after all talk had been exhausted downstairs in the sitting room. Hours of discussion hadn't established anything new or helpful in terms of resolving the situation, and he found he simply had to get away from it all. So here he was, alone at last, pacing the long hall that served as the informal gallery at the abbey. Alain had come by once ostensibly to see if he needed any food or drink, but Giles had sensed he'd come to talk things over once again, to be a supportive friend if need be. Giles, while grateful for the offer, had turned him away.

He knew Alain and Tristan had strategies and plans. Most likely those plans would secure Spelthorne for him and shut off any further avenue of pursuit Cate might take. However, this tangle was something he had to resolve on his own, in his own way. What Alain and

Tristan didn't see or perhaps didn't fully recognize was the emotional layer beneath the legal surface. There was a family, a history at stake here.

He paused before his father's portrait, an elegant oil done in the tradition of Joshua Reynolds. It was difficult to reshape his viewing of it. This was not a picture of his father but of the man he'd *believed* was his father, right up until that morning. The man in the portrait was in his full prime, perhaps thirty-five years of age, not much older than Giles was now. His hair was glossy and golden, his eyes intelligent if hard in their shrewd assessment of the world they viewed. He was outfitted in the best of fashion at the turn of the century.

Giles had been told throughout his growing up how much he resembled his father physically and in mannerisms. He had both warmed to those compliments and quietly rebelled against them. His father had been a man Giles had respected at a distance. An earl had responsibilities to people that superseded obligations to a family or to a single son. As much as Giles would have preferred more time with his father growing up, he had been taught not to expect it. As he grew older, he often found himself thankful for that early lesson.

Watching the deteriorating marriage between his parents, he understood that his father was incapable of establishing close attachments. He was coldly courteous to Giles's mother but nothing more even though her adoration and attempts to reconcile with him were painfully obvious. Giles had believed and feared that he was like his father in that regard.

That fear became a double-edged sword as he entered his twenties and entered the world of the *ton*. As the scion to a prestigious title, he was expected to have his *affaires de coeur* while he sowed his oats and looked for a respectable wife. Fearing that he lacked the ability to have a meaningful relationship, Giles did not let himself put it to the test. Thus he'd arrived at the age of thirty, still unattached, still looking for a grand passion. Of course, he was still in the process of realizing that if this man wasn't his father, then he might indeed be capable of loving most intensely.

Light footsteps sounded at the gallery entrance. Giles resisted turning around. The footfalls indicated it wasn't Alain or Tristan. He worried they'd conspired to send Bella. He wasn't ready for her either.

"Giles."

It was Cate. He wondered if Tristan had driven her from their presence. If so, she'd be devastated. He didn't have to be told how much Cate had come to rely on the guidance of Bella and Cecile over the past weeks. Losing them would hurt her although she'd have to have known the loss of their friendship was inevitable under the circumstances.

He turned to face her. One glance at her face told him all he needed to know. She was suffering too. He was suddenly glad she'd been the one to come. She was the one he needed to be with. Any resolution could come only from them. He'd decided early in his pacing that there were certain stratagems he would not embrace. He held out his hand to her, inviting her to join him on the low bench against the long windows opposite the portraits.

"Am I intruding?" Cate asked quietly.

"No," Giles tendered a brief smile. "Did they run you off?"

Cate shook her head. "No. Your friends are far too well-bred for that. But I sensed their unease and went to my rooms shortly after you left. However," she paused here and pleated the skirt of her gown between her fingers, "I found I needed to talk with you, alone. I have made decisions during the course of the afternoon but they are useless without your collaboration."

Giles nodded. "I think that is very wise. I have made decisions too. Yet, I feel that any true decision must be made between us, together."

"We must not act hastily. Perhaps the span of an afternoon after an emotional morning is not enough time," Cate offered hesitantly.

"It's been more than an afternoon of thought, Cate. I feel as if I've thought of nothing else for the last four weeks. This situation has been on my mind constantly. I've spent hours and hours turning over options until my contingencies have contingencies." Giles gave a soft self-deprecating laugh.

"Of course you did. I would expect nothing less from you." Cate smiled at him, a bit of mischief sparking in her green eyes. The sight of it warmed him and Giles felt relaxed, at ease. He leaned back against the window pane and stared at his father's portrait.

"It's hard to imagine he's not my father." There, he said it out loud, the thing that had sat heaviest on his heart that afternoon as he paced. He felt Cate's hand lace with his own where it lay upon his leg. Her hand felt warm, comforting as it linked with his.

"He was your father, Giles, just not in the usual way we are conditioned to think of them. He taught you about being a man, how to be his heir."

Giles nodded. "I suppose he did, although I cannot say I'm grateful for all the things he taught me. I also learned a great many things I did not want to aspire to by watching him."

"I suspect that is true for most children." Cate laughed. "I don't know anyone who wants to be an exact replica of their parents." Then she sobered. "I certainly don't want to be like my mother. I would like to think I could not have done what she did. It scares me to think what loving a man could drive me to."

"When I think of my mother," Giles said slowly, "I sometimes wonder if she had ever been stable. I was too young to understand what it was that happened between her and father. But she had intense mood swings. She would go through alternate periods of doting on me and then ignoring me altogether."

"Magda never ignored me. She devoted herself to me wholeheartedly when she could have easily chosen to do otherwise."

"Of course she did. You were her ticket to security," Giles ground out.

"Giles! Don't be unkind. It wasn't like that. Besides,

even if that was her motive, I can't believe it. She's all the family I've got."

"You've got the Moncriefs." Giles waved a hand at the line of portraits.

"They're not really my family any more than the cottager who birthed you."

"Then why did you come seeking to associate yourself with them?" Giles challenged, shifting his position to look squarely at her, removing his hand from hers.

"I liked the idea of it," Cate said softly. "But it's not all I thought it would be and at the same time, it's a great deal more than I thought it would be. Which is why I've made some decisions. I would like you to hear them now."

Giles nodded. "I would prefer to go first."

"Fine. I am ready to listen." She settled herself on the bench, tucking her skirts about her legs so that she could draw her knees up and rest her chin on them.

Giles rose and began pacing the short length of the bench. "It is apparent to me, based on Vicar Waring's news this morning that there is some question as to the legitimate heir of Spelthorne. That question can either be decided privately between the two of us, or it can be decided publicly in the court of law with all the attendant scandal that will accompany it." Here, Giles paused to watch Cate weigh his words. "You are an intelligent woman, Cate. I do not think you actually believe you could win in a court of law against a peer of my standing." He saw her start to stiffen at the claim, her temper rising in her eyes. He held up his hand to stall her protest.

"I don't mean this pompously, Cate. I mean to counsel you on the realities of your choices," he pleaded, softening his tone to convince her of his sincerity. "There are enough suppositions I can make to weaken your case. The emerald may have been stolen. Perhaps Magda took it when she visited here years ago. Perhaps there was a daughter but that daughter was not you." Giles shook his head. "You heard all the arguments this morning. I have no desire to repeat them here or in a court of law. I do not want to see you hurt. Taking this to a public trial would not only hurt you but endanger you. You could be convicted of fraud, of playing an imposter."

The look on her face was one of shock.

"Didn't you know?"

Cate shook her head wearily. "I didn't stop to think about those consequences."

Giles nodded. "It is understandable, but there it is. I cannot allow you to take that risk when I feel certain that you would be outmanned, outgunned, out-maneuvered on all fronts regardless of the truth."

Cate's head came up at that. "The truth?"

Giles sat down next to her, taking her hands. "I have no intention of relinquishing Spelthorne but I do acknowledge privately to you and only to you, that the story you tell is very likely the truth. You may be Spelthorne's heir, but I am Spelthorne's earl. To me, as I paced the gallery this afternoon, that is the only issue that needs resolving. How can the heir and the earl be reconciled without scandal, without one or the other being harmed but with them both attaining their goals?"

"I want to tell you of the decision I made, before you go any further," Cate cut in. "I want you to know so that whatever you say or do after this point, you do so knowing my full mind and knowing that you were not manipulated or misled," She insisted with a quiet fervor. "I believe fully that I am the rightful heir, that I was given away at birth, and that a boy was put in my place. But I do not seek to supplant you. I would be foolish to think I could run this estate, that I could command the loyalty and respect of all those who look to you for leadership. Spelthorne needs you."

Giles inclined his head in a slight bow. "I thank you for that compliment. It seems that we are agreed on our perception of the problem that lies before us. This may make my plan more palatable to you."

The afternoon shadows were lengthening when Giles went down on one buff trousered knee before her and took her hand, which he noticed trembled beneath his own. "For the sake of all the reasons known and unknown, for the sake of creating rightness out of an unjust situation, I am asking you to marry me, to be by my side as my countess."

The look on her face was inscrutable in the failing light of the afternoon. Giles would have given a hundred guineas to know what she was thinking as she struggled to take in his words.

The proposal had come, just as Magda had said it would. Magda had believed such an alliance was inevitable, the only solution that could privately resolve the issue. Cate was stunned. She'd tried to forestall it, even prevent it with her plan. She'd thought by telling him she would not seek to put him off Spelthorne he'd feel relieved of any obligation to sacrifice himself upon the altar of matrimony.

She should have seen sooner that Giles Moncrief didn't work that way. He was a man of honor and his honor demanded the alliance. At least the proposal had been truthful. He had not made any false protestations of love or shower her with meaningless romantic poetry about her eyes or her hair. And why should he? He was not courting her. He was paying her what she was owed in the only currency available to him since she'd already so resolutely refused his offer of money.

Magda would be ecstatic. But Magda didn't have to live with him the rest of her life. Magda didn't have to live with her conscience, knowing what had driven him to make the proposal. In truth, she was smart enough to know that he was proposing to Spelthorne, not to her.

She had to say something. The silence was stretching out to an embarrassing length. "You don't have to do this," she stammered. "Surely there must be another way."

"Do you know of one?" Giles reprimanded her softly. "If there was, I would have found it by now."

Cate gave an unladylike snort. "For that reason, I must respectfully decline your well-meant proposal."

"Don't be foolish, Cate. Your refusal condemns us both," Giles warned. "If I lavished sweet words on you, you'd know I was lying. I will not commit the mistakes of my father by pretending to something that isn't there, simply to win my bride." There was an edge to his voice.

Cate answered the challenge. "I am thirty-years old, like yourself, Giles. I am no young debutante full of romantic notions. I am full of practicalities. I do not think it would be much of a life shackled to a man with the knowledge that I'd coerced him to the point of offering for me."

His next words surprised her. "Do you think it would be like that, Cate? Do you truly believe there is no hope for us? Certainly, we are not in love at this moment, but we've had no chance to explore that. We've shared the briefest of kisses and yet you cannot deny there is passion between us." He bent his lips to her hand and pressed a kiss in her open palm. His lips trailed a line of hot kisses to her wrist and upward to her elbow in reminder of the kisses that had gone before.

Cate gasped. Her skin flamed beneath his touch, instantly ignited by his caress. "Giles, please . . . I don't know. I can't think when you do this." Cate sighed, wanting to give herself up to caress of his hand on the nape of her neck, to the promises made in his eyes, midnight-dark with desire.

"Then say yes, Cate."

For reasons that had little to do with Spelthorne and everything to do with the possibilities promised in his kiss, she did.

Chapter Thirteen

Giles announced their betrothal that evening at supper. It almost felt real when he'd stood at the end of the meal and raised his wine glass in a toast to his impending nuptials. He gave her a warm glance that she imagined a happy betrothed might give his intended. There, all similarity ended. Alain and Tristan made no attempt to hide their shock. Isabella and Cecile had smiled and done a better job of masking their surprise. The two women artfully pre-empted the arguments on their husbands' lips with lively chatter about the wedding. Isabella rose and immediately excused the women to the drawing room, declaring they had plans to make.

In the drawing room, Cate hadn't known what to make of all of Isabella's conversation. The countess had asked several questions about the wedding: when would it take place? Where would it be held? Cate felt awkward. She didn't know and the countess was carrying on as if this were to be the social event of the year. Surely, Isabella knew better than that. Cate let her talk until Giles and the gentlemen joined them after their port.

Isabella wasted no time turning her questions on Giles. That was when Cate had gleaned that Giles wanted the wedding immediately, the day after next. Isabella was scandalized and argued him into waiting five days. She'd wanted a week or two but Giles insisted the marriage take place quickly. Five days, he said, was more than enough time to procure a marriage license from the village clergyman and to make some minimal arrangements. Nothing more was needed.

Cate felt her cheeks flush at his brusque manner. What he really meant was that no arrangements were needed for a wedding such as this. It was quite a telling comment from a man who was famed for his entertainments and organizational abilities. It might be true that little fuss was needed over such a hasty and arranged marriage, but still Giles might have put a better face on it.

Isabella leapt into the breach left by his comment. "Shame on you, Giles. All haste and reason aside, every bride deserves a bit of fussing. All wedding days are special in their own way." She smiled to soften her scolding. "Cate needs a dress at the very least, and I haven't anything suitable on hand for a wedding gown. We'll need time to create something worthy of the occasion. We'll barely have time to send to the Meadows for Tristan's roses to decorate the chapel with."

From that moment forward, Isabella and Cecile dominated her schedule with plans. The next morning, Cate found herself inundated with lists and questions. At mid-morning, Giles saved her with an offer to walk her over to the old Norman chapel at Spelthorne where the ceremony would be held.

The little church had character aplenty and was in good repair since services were regularly held in there on Sunday afternoons for those who didn't attend the larger, newer church in the village which had been built when Spelthorne's population exceeded the capacity of the little chapel. Giles stood in the archway of the nave, watching her expectantly while she strolled the length of the aisle. "Will it do, Cate? I should have asked what you would prefer. We can have the ceremony at the abbey or at the village church if you'd like."

Cate stopped her idle progress to face him. "What do *you* prefer, Giles? If you'd rather not marry in a church, we can do it quietly in the drawing room at the abbey."

Giles pulled off his gloves and slapped them in the palm of one hand. "A wedding is a proud moment for a woman. I was thoughtless last night in the drawing room. I am sorry. I did not mean to devalue the ceremony or you."

Cate smiled, suppressing a laugh. "A wedding is a proud moment for a woman? Only the woman? What about the man? Isn't it a crowning moment for him too? I can see that I shall have to reform you immediately. A man should be proud he's found a helpmate, a woman who will be loyal and stand beside him." She paused in her teasing. No doubt, Giles had hoped to find those things in a mate but probably felt she would not live up to those standards.

She bit her lip and moved toward him, taking the liberty of placing her hand on her betrothed's sleeve. It was a novel experience to think of him as her betrothed, to think she could approach him as she did, at least in private. "This marriage might not be what you'd anticipated for yourself, but I can be all those things. I mean to be loyal to you, Giles. I mean to be your helpmate if you'll teach me, if you'll let me."

She looked up into his blue eyes, seeking an affirmation. He gave her a slight nod. "We shall both do our best," he said with more reserve than Cate would have liked.

"This place is fine for the ceremony, quite charming actually," Cate said, reverting to the earlier topic of conversation. It would be charming in the spring. In her mind's eye, she saw the bleak stone chapel decked out for a spring wedding, full of wildflowers and garlands, a pristine cloth on the altar. But at the end of fall, when winter stood on the cusp, it looked cold and gray. She hoped it wasn't a foreshadowing of her marriage.

"Are you ready to go back? There's something I want to show you up at the house." Giles offered her his arm, and they began the walk back to the abbey. On the way back, he played the part of the solicitous bridegroom to the hilt, asking after the plans and lists Isabella had concocted.

He laughed out loud as Cate recounted the morning

spent with Isabella. "Gracious! You'd think from the way she's carrying on this was a society ball. Don't let her overwhelm you. She's a dear friend and good at her job. She's one of London's finest hostesses when she and Tristan endeavor to go up to town. But don't let her talk you into anything you don't want."

His banter and agreement with her was heartening. Cate felt a few moments of kinship with him then. Perhaps they would build a future on conversations like this one, a little bit at a time.

As they neared the abbey, Giles said, "I am glad you liked the little chapel. I always thought I'd be married there. It's the place where all the earls have been married and buried. The graveyard off to the side is where our ancestors are laid. It's where I'll be laid to rest when my time comes and you as well. There's some comfort and peace in knowing how one fits into the cycle of life."

"Hmm," Cate said dreamily, taking in the chance to view Spelthorne through his eyes. Another might have found his comment of death linked with marriage morbidly inappropriate, but she understood the connection. "I think that is why I found the idea of Spelthorne so appealing. It represented peace, rest, security, all of which are absent qualities in the life of the Rom. I've discovered I don't uproot well. Traveling, moving around, is not part of my make-up."

She peered up at him, thinking of something else he'd said. "You said 'our.' "

"Yes. It occurred to me last night that although you

don't know your ancestors they are your people, your blood. The Spelthorne earls go back four generations. You are the great-granddaughter of James Moncrief. Although I am not of their blood, I am of their traditions as well. As you said yesterday, there are many ways to be a father. If so, I think there are many ways to be part of the family history."

"I think you're right," Cate said softly, feeling some of the guilt over their marriage lifting from her. Giles was coming to terms with his new understanding of his identity, just as she was coming to grips with hers.

Once they reached the house, the quiet peace they'd shared on the walk back was shattered. Isabella met them in the hall, a sheaf of paper in her hand. "Giles, there you are! There's been a set back." She brandished the paper.

Giles gave Cate a conspiratorial wink and Cate could see his mouth twitch as he tried to suppress a laugh.

"It's not funny in the least!" Isabella stormed. "When you pick a wedding day, you usually consult a calendar."

Cate looked from Giles to Isabella, perplexed.

"Do you know that five days from yesterday is All Hallows' Eve?" Isabella said, her disbelief over his carelessness evident in her tone.

Giles couldn't suppress his laughter any longer. "No, I didn't. But I would like to say that I was badgered into five days by you, Bella. If it had been up to me, I would have been married tomorrow. All Hallows' Eve it is. We can marry in an evening ceremony."

"Evening? That's positively medieval. When have

fashionable people wed at night? What about a wedding breakfast?" Isabella protested.

"When they're me." Giles merely smiled, unbothered by her well-meaning protestations. "Now, I was off to show Cate something upstairs." He turned back to her and tugged on her hand, leading her upstairs with a playfulness in his step.

Upstairs turned out to be the attics. These rooms were unlike any attic Cate had been in, although admittedly, that was very few. The attics were a warren of gabled rooms at the top of the house filled with treasures. She could have spent hours wandering through them. Unlike her perception of an attic, these rooms were well organized, nothing was crammed in haphazardly and items appeared as if they had been stored with great care, in spite of the expected layers of dust which accumulated with lack of use.

Giles proudly announced that one of the things he'd done since becoming the earl was to catalog the contents of the attics. The idea of Giles crawling about the rooms in his impeccable clothing, writing down the items made her giggle.

"If you think that is funny," Giles shot her a mocking glare, "I am currently beginning to write the history of each item. Its year or origin, which relative it belonged to, and what purpose or history is behind it. You can help me with it. It would be a great project for getting to know your family." He paused. "By the way, why is cataloging funny? It happens to be a great historical resource."

He looked so self-righteous, Cate couldn't help herself from blurting out the truth. "I can't imagine you in your very proper clothing up here in the dust, rummaging through trunks holding who knows what."

Giles looked serious and vulnerable. Perhaps she had gone too far. She should have realized they didn't know each other well enough for such disclosures yet. "Is that how you see me? Too proper? Too much a gentleman to dirty his hands with work?"

She *had* hurt his feelings. "No, of course not. I am sorry."

"For what? For telling me the truth?"

Cate wrung her hands, searching for a way to make things right. "The truth is, I like the way you dress. It was one of the first things I noticed about you, what made you stand out from other gentlemen. The way you look in your clothes is quite handsome." She lowered her voice to a coquette's whisper and dared a little, "The way you look out of your clothing is quite admirable too."

That won her a smile and a chuckle. "Ho! Out of my clothes you say? Have you been spying on me?"

"No, but I have been fishing with you."

That made them both laugh. Cate was reassured. They were indeed building a history together, one conversation, one experience, one day at a time.

"Here it is," Giles called out, gesturing to a trunk that was set out from the rest toward the back of the garret. "I couldn't sleep last night so I came up here to search for some items I recalled from my cataloging. Thanks to my excellent record keeping, I was able to locate the trunk right away," he added pointedly, winning another laugh from Cate.

She came to stand beside him and stared down at the big, scarred traveling trunk with iron bands. "The trunk looks ancient. What's in there? Spanish doubloons?"

"Better than Spanish gold." Giles winked and lifted the lid.

The smell of lavender and cedar chips wafted out from the open trunk. Cate felt her curiosity build at the scent. The trunk was exquisitely lined in ruched satin and there was no doubt that this trunk had belonged to a woman of means.

Giles rubbed at an engraved plate embedded in the lid of the trunk. "It's my great-grandmother's—our great grandmother's. There's her name, Heloise."

"The one married to James?" Cate asked.

"Yes. You're learning," Giles smiled.

He dug down into the layers of tissue and wrapping. "She and great-grandfather were married in the little chapel in 1680." He drew out a bundle. "This is the gown she wore for her wedding."

The layers of wrapping came off, and Cate gasped. The gown Giles uncovered was of sapphire silk, cut in the fashion of the period with the rounded neckline, exposing the shoulders and the bodice tapering to a vee, not unlike the royal red gown she'd worn to dinner a few nights previous. The gown was trimmed in exquisite lace work at the sleeves and the low neck. "It's beautiful." Cate couldn't resist the urge to finger it.

"I thought of it after seeing your red gown," Giles said. "The style suited you well. I thought you might like to wear this for our wedding." He shrugged. "It certainly fits the rhyme about something old, something borrowed, something blue."

Cate could barely find any words to respond. "Really? I could wear it?"

"If you'd like. There are other gowns up here. Celeste's is here if you would prefer . . ." Giles's voice broke off.

"No," Cate said quickly, "this is the one."

"The women can alter it in anyway you need. I am sorry there's not more time. I want you to have a suitable dress."

"Thank you," Cate said reverently. "This dress will more than suffice."

The day of the wedding dawned wet and gray, not exactly the type of weather one imagined when thinking of the ideal wedding. Then again, there was nothing "ideal" about the wedding that would take place later that day. Cate dropped the curtain and sighed, curling up on the window seat in her customary position.

Across the room, the dress hung ready, along with an elegant ermine-lined hooded cloak and matching slippers Giles had dug out of the trunk along with the gown. Eight hours separated her from that gown.

For better or for worse, Cate had no doubts that the day would pass quickly enough. Giles's friends had filled the wedding day with activities. She would have to hurry and dress in order to be ready to help with the decorating of the chapel, which would take up the morning. Then Isabella had something planned with the village ladies that Cate had no idea about but Giles had seemed to approve so she had not protested, wanting to make him happy in return for the generosity he'd shown her.

True to expectation, the morning flew by in a festive manner as the six of them devoted their efforts to the chapel, along with the household staff at the abbey.

When they were finished, Cate had to recant all her previous thoughts about the chapel appearing dreary. Their efforts had transformed the bleakness into a backdrop from another time.

The season had made it difficult to come up with the flora and fauna that would have been available during the spring and summer. Isabella had improvised with ribbons, and Giles had unearthed a trunk filled with carpets from James and Heloise's time. One of those carpets served as a runner down the short aisle. Another acted as a tapestry backdrop, skillfully hung behind the altar. Isabella's ribbons roped off the pews from the center aisle so that guests would enter down the right and left sides of the church. Large, tapers were placed in the niche of each stained-glass window and in profusion around the altar. Two large vases of exquisite red roses graced the front of the chapel. In the candlelight of evening, it would look magical.

Returning home to the abbey, Cate found the village women and wives of the tenant farmers assembled in the drawing room, awaiting her arrival over a lavish tea. Isabella hastily explained it was a chance for the women to celebrate her coming into their ranks as a new addition to the female community of Spelthorne.

Cate realized she knew many of them as Isabella walked about the room with her, making introductions. She had indeed met several of them on her afternoon outings with Giles.

Once the introductions were complete and she was settled in the seat of honor on the settee, the clergyman's wife spoke up. "Here at Spelthorne, we have a custom of giving advice to new wives. Each of us has brought a gift and some advice to go with it." There was general laughter and tittering at the implications, and Cate felt her cheeks heat.

By the end of the afternoon, a pile of gifts ranging from handstitched pillowcases to a gauzy, frothy nightgown from Isabella, lay at her feet.

The ladies left and their departure left a stillness hanging over the abbey, anticipation was running high. Isabella and Cecile ushered her upstairs for a bath and some time alone. Her last time alone, she realized. From now on, she'd be sharing a chamber with her husband. Already, looking about her room, it was evident that the household staff had been busy moving her items while the party had been going on downstairs. Only her wedding gown and toilet items remained.

To her surprise, Cate did find the ability to rest before her bath and eat a little from the tray brought up to her. By the time the maid returned to help her into the gown, she felt like a bride. All of her attention was focused on the impending ceremony, of seeing her husband standing at the front of the church, of saying vows and meaning them. She was scared and excited all at once, all thoughts of how this moment had come to pass were driven from her mind at least temporarily.

Downstairs an open carriage waited to transport her to the chapel. The rain had stopped at midday and the dark sky twinkled overhead with stars. Lanterns posted on the carriage front lit the path for the short journey. Isabella and Cecile rode with her, and Alain rode beside them. Tristan waited at the chapel with Giles. There was a hubbub as they neared the church, and Cate realized suddenly that there would be guests. She had assumed the ceremony would be attended simply by Giles and his friends.

"Where did all these people come from?" Cate whispered to Isabella.

"From the village," Isabella said, confused at the question. "Did you think there wouldn't be any guests to see their earl married?"

"Actually, no," she admitted honestly.

Alain rode on ahead to announce the bride was arriving and the last of the guests made their way inside. From outdoors Cate could see the tapers shining in through the windows and it struck her anew that this was her wedding.

"We'll see you inside." Isabella and Cecile squeezed her hand and took up their places. Alain came to help her down from the carriage and keep her out of the mud.

Inside, Cate had to pause a moment to keep herself from crying. The chapel was full, the candles cast a romantic glow on the walls and, best of all, Giles waited for her at the end of the aisle, standing straight, and immaculate in black evening attire, his hair gleaming golden in the candlelight, her own handsome prince. This was a moment for fairy tales. Then Cecile stood up and began to play softly on her violin.

The aisle seemed longer now that she had to walk it with everyone looking on. She was glad for the reassuring pressure of Giles's hand on hers when she arrived at the front, happy to have gotten there without tripping.

Later she would not remember much of the actual ceremony—just images of candles and stained glass, the scent of roses, the sound of Cecile's music, and the blurred background voice of the clergyman intoning the words that would bind her to this man that she knew well and yet not well at all. But the one thing that remained always clear to her was the moment Giles sealed their union with his kiss and led her back down the aisle as his wife and into her new life.

Chapter Fourteen

Giles rushed Cate down the aisle in a half run through a gauntlet of well wishers raining them with fragrant rose petals. The weather and the lateness of the ceremony would not allow for the guests to shower the wedded couple out of doors, so it had been arranged to follow the customary tradition indoors.

Cate suspected Cecile and Isabella had plotted it without Giles's knowledge. Everyone was laughing and in high spirits as she and Giles passed down the aisle. Even Giles seemed exuberant. He'd been serious when he'd spoken his vows but now he squeezed her hand affectionately and paused in the archway of the church to look back over the guests, an extraordinary smile wreathing his face.

Giles swung her into his arms, causing her to stifle a

little shriek of surprise and treated the villagers to the sight of a dramatic kiss. They cheered loudly and he reached for a leather bag that had been left at the back of the church on a small table. Opening its drawstring neck, he drew out a handful of coins and tossed them high into the air, another custom that had to be followed when the lord of the manor married.

Everyone made a show of madly scrambling for the coins. Alain took over after that, flinging the remaining handfuls while they made a quick get-away to the waiting carriage. Giles swept Cate up and saw her tucked safely inside before climbing in beside her.

He stared at her intensely as the carriage started the short drive to the abbey. "How are you, Mrs. Moncrief? Or do you prefer Lady Spelthorne?" He teased in high humor.

"I am fine, more than fine," Cate confessed, knowing that tears glimmered in her eyes. "I can't believe that was my wedding. It was so beautiful. I never imagined . . ." She was at a loss for words. "Everyone did so much for me and they don't even know me."

"The night's not over yet. Wait until you see what's at the abbey." Giles's eyes twinkled in anticipation.

Cate heard music as soon as the carriage turned into the drive. Not orchestra music or the refined music that had played at Giles's house party ball, but to her mind, "real" music. Music with fiddles, drums, and tambourines. The music of the countryside.

A bonfire burned large and bright in the courtyard,

warming the cold night. The doors of the house were thrown open. Cate saw immediately what Giles had planned.

"A real All Souls night!" She clapped her hands in delight.

Already, villagers who had stayed behind to make everything ready were dancing to a polka. Giles jumped down from the carriage and helped her out.

Cate beamed, letting Giles sweep her into the dancers.

The night was filled with dancing and drink and food on groaning trestle tables set up out of doors. The fire and the dancing kept everyone warm although there was access to the house for those who could not stomach the cold night. Cate was exhilarated and giddy with the excitement of the party. It was the perfect way to celebrate the wedding among the Spelthorne peoples— a tribute to old England as it was in the days of the first earl, James Moncrief.

Eventually, it was time to end it, at least their participation in it. Giles offered one last toast to his bride and made a great show of lifting her in his arms and carrying her across the threshold of the abbey. The crowd roared its approval. They would stay outside and continue their merrymaking as long as they wished.

Tristan, Alain, and their wives followed them in. Giles set her down gently and gave her a light kiss. "You've made me a happy man tonight, Cate. I'll take one last drink with Tristan and Alain, and then I shall come to you." He lifted her hand and kissed her knuckles in a gallant gesture that made her tremble in anticipation.

Isabella and Cecile came upstairs with her and played at maids, helping her out of the lovely gown and setting it safely aside to be stored away for another generation. To their credit, they didn't stay long and were well gone before Giles made his appearance.

Cate liked Giles's friends well enough, considering the circumstances surrounding their befriendment of her, but she wanted these next few moments to be between she and Giles alone. Ever since she'd appeared at Spelthorne and laid her claims at Giles's doorstep, the two of them had been surrounded by people. First, the house party guests and then the constant presence of his four close friends. Now, it was time just for them.

Giles opened the bedroom door. "Are we alone?" he asked, unknowingly echoing her sentiments.

She smiled as he pulled at his cravat, unraveling the complicated knots he liked to wear. "Absolutely, completely and utterly alone."

The grin on his face was part rake and part happy bridegroom. "Finally, I shall have you to myself at last."

She went to him and pulled him close. "The future starts now—our future, Giles Moncrief."

"Indeed, it does." Giles cupped the back of her head in his hand and bent to claim a deep kiss, smiling as he did so. Cate gave herself over to it.

She would not wonder until much later how simply won her happiness and Giles's had been once they'd decided to wed. In the five days since the afternoon of Giles's proposal, obstacles had vanished and talk over her legitimacy had ceased. Life had gotten smoother. If she hadn't been so enthralled with her new husband's passionate attentions, she would have recognized sooner that it had all been too easy.

Marriage agreed with him, most definitely, Giles decided over the next few days. He looked up from the papers he was reading on his desk three days later to savor Cate's presence feet away from him on the settee.

They were enjoying the quiet of a deserted Spelthorne Abbey. Tristan and Alain had discreetly packed themselves and their families off to their homes for the holidays, leaving the newlyweds on their own—something Giles was exceedingly grateful for. He wanted to thoroughly bask in the serenity that currently claimed his life.

Giles was fully aware that Cate was the source of the contentment that surrounded him these last days. His mind was no longer whirring with a thousand plans and a hundred worries. Spelthorne was safe. The claims against him and his legitimacy had been thoroughly scotched with the marriage.

He had done his duty for Spelthorne, although in a most unconventional way. Most gentlemen he knew did their titular duties by marrying a wife of fine pedigree. He'd done his duty by doing the opposite. He had Cate to thank for that.

Cate looked up from the book she was reading and caught him staring. "What are you thinking?"

Giles laughed at having been caught. "I am thinking how beautiful my wife is and how much more lovely she'll be when she has clothes of her own. We can't have you wearing Bella's gowns forever." He'd won Spelthorne and in exchange, she'd won a new life—a life he'd gladly lead her into. It would be his first gift to her. His lovely new bride would need an entire wardrobe. He could help her see to an appropriate country wardrobe here at Spelthorne well enough but they'd need to go up to London and do her town wardrobe there.

Time enough for that after the Christmas holidays. Strangely enough, he had no desire to go haring up to town for the Michelmas session of parliament. The House of Lords would have to do without him this year for the first time since he'd assumed the title. The thought of a country Christmas at Spelthorne with Cate made him grin up at the ceiling. He was looking forward to sharing all the traditions with her. This year, there would be a very personal meaning for him of peace on earth.

"I have news." Lady Fox-Haughton's latest protégé said casually, leaning his well-polished boots against the fender of her fireplace.

She threw a pointed glance at the ill-placed boots and he hastily removed them. The man was handsome enough with his broad shoulders and Norse good looks but breeding was lacking. That's what happened when one had to settle for a third son of an earl out of Sussex.

Splitting with Giles had left a sour taste in her mouth after she'd returned to London in the fall. In hindsight, she supposed she'd been too quick to pick a new apprentice.

She scoffed. Apprentice was not a word she'd ever have chosen to use to describe Giles, but the word definitely fit the young Norse god lounging in her parlor. At least this man could be taught, and he wasn't astute enough to have his own views. When she wanted his opinion, she gave it to him.

"You said you had news?" she prompted.

"Yes. Spelthorne won't be coming up to town for the Michelmas session."

"Not coming?" Candice hid her surprise. Such an action wasn't like Giles at all. He was always so overly responsible. Not even her vaunted skills could pry him away from parliament when he had an issue on the floor for discussion.

"Indeed. Rumor has it he has married and is spending Christmas in the country as a winter honeymoon of sorts with his new bride." He delivered the last bit with a smug cockiness, knowing that for once he knew something she didn't.

"Wipe that look off your face. I would have heard it tonight," Candice rallied. "If you really know something, you know her name."

"Jealous are we?" he asked, piqued at her set down. "Wishing you had Spelthorne back?"

Candice snapped her fingers. "If I wanted Spelthorne back, I'd have him. He wasn't as promising as I'd hoped." She gave him a meaningful look to say that the same thing could happen to him. Then she sat down and picked up a newspaper, ignoring him entirely. It wouldn't do to look too eager for the name of Giles's bride.

She let Daniel fidget uncomfortably for a few minutes, knowing the hothead wouldn't be able to contain himself.

She covertly looked at the clock. Within five minutes she'd have the name if he knew it.

On cue, Daniel stood up and began pacing. "Don't you want to know?"

"Know what, dear?" she said sweetly, as if their spat hadn't happened.

"Her name?"

"Only if you know it. I was under the impression you didn't know it."

"Of course I know it! I didn't leave the club until I had all the information available. What do you take me for? Spelthorne has married his fourth cousin, Cate Winthrop." He gave a derisive snort. "I would have thought a man like Spelthorne could have done better than marrying some poor distant relation none of us have heard of. Poor sot."

The last had been said more to himself than to any audience, but Lady Fox-Haughton picked up on it immediately. "Are you sure?" She was all attention, her mind firing quickly.

"Quite sure."

She strode to the shelve where she kept her important reference books and pulled out her well-used copy of *DeBrett's Peerage*. She thumbed through the pages until she found what she was looking for. She hadn't given it much thought upon her return over a month ago, but now it suddenly seemed of pre-eminent importance since Giles had gone and married the girl.

"Ha! He couldn't have married Cate Winthrop because she doesn't exist." Candice moved her finger through the Winthrop lineage. "She'd have to be the daughter of Stonebridge's younger brother's son to be a fourth cousin," she muttered, scanning the lines to make sure she didn't overlook anything. "Ha! There is a C. Winthrop but it's a child who died in infancy and my copy doesn't denote if it was male or female."

Daniel looked perplexed, a furrowing marring his smooth brow. "Then how can he have married her?"

Candice slammed the book shut with an impressive bang. "He didn't marry her. He married someone pretending to be her." She tapped a hand on the table, thinking fast. "The question is, does Giles know? Perhaps someone is hoodwinking him or perhaps they are in it together and they want us to believe that is who she is." Now why would Giles, the most ethical man she knew, try to perpetrate a scheme that was bound to fail? Surely everyone would know there was no such person as Cate Winthrop?

"Daniel, I need you to do something for me, darling. I need you to get a look at that marriage certificate. Whose name is on it? I'll wager it's not Cate Winthrop's."

Chapter Fourteen

Spelthorne Abbey, December 24th

"Wake up, sleepyhead!" Cate shouted, throwing back the heavy draperies cloaking the master chamber windows in floor-to-ceiling elegance. A burst of rare winter sunlight filled the room. "It's time!"

In the bed, Giles groaned and threw a hand across his eyes. She laughed in satisfaction. She'd risen early on purpose to tease him. Usually, he was the first one up and he loved to rib her over her penchant for sleeping in. Today she'd bested him.

It hadn't been that difficult. Her excitement over the impending holiday had propelled her from bed early.

She tugged on the satin comforter and threw it back. Giles groaned again. "What's so special about today?" he yawned.

"What's so special about today?" she said in mock disbelief, hearing the teasing tone in his voice despite his complaints. "It's Christmas Eve!" Her first Christmas as a married woman and in some ways her first Christmas ever. Never had she spent a Christmas surrounded by the activities that had the abbey already bustling at dawn. This morning the abbey and all who wanted to come were going out to fetch the greenery and the yule log. Tonight there'd be a grand party, and later a quiet church service in the little Norman chapel.

Giles smiled widely, something he'd done more often since their marriage. He reached up his hands to grasp hers. "Is it too early to say Merry Christmas?"

Cate giggled, sensing his excitement too. "You'll have to hurry; people are already gathering in the stable yard. They await their lord. Shall you get up, or shall I tell them to go a-greening without him?"

Giles sprung out of bed in a fluid motion. "I'll be ready in a moment's notice."

She flashed him a final smile before going downstairs to wait for him. She'd come to treasure spontaneous moments like these when they were alone, not surrounded by the servants or the demands of earldom.

It was those moments where she learned the most about Giles the man, who he was apart from being the embodiment of Spelthorne. She had not known him before their marriage, but in their brief acquaintance before the wedding, she'd deduced he was a man of great responsibilities, someone on who others relied. He took those responsibilities seriously, leaving little time for himself to relax and set those burdens down. These days, she thought he did a bit more of that—for the better. He laughed easily, smiled, played, found a certain exuberance in doing the everyday tasks required of him.

He had shown her every courtesy a man could show his wife. She was overly conscious of the fact that he never treated her with anything less than the honor she deserved as his partner. He was sincere in his regard and tender in his affections. In short, he was as much a paragon of a husband as he was an earl.

Although she knew the grounds upon which he'd offered for her, she also knew she was dangerously close to falling in desperate love with her new husband. In spite of their rocky start, there was no reason not too. And perhaps that was what held her back from pledging the very last piece of her heart that was not already his.

He was too perfect. He'd accepted his situation with equanimity. Not once had he ranted over having to take a wife that was beneath him or that there was the intangible taint of blackmail surrounding his proposal. He'd simply made the best of it and forged ahead.

Perfection and the attainment of happy-ever-after were not part of the hard life she'd known with the gypsies. Cate worried about accepting the smooth reality Giles's life laid at her feet. She was convinced all she'd found with him would eventually be obliterated. Some day the carpet would be pulled out from under her and the reality beneath the illusions of their life would be cruel—even heartbreaking if she let them. So she did her best to protect herself against the coming of that day.

But it was a hard task, one she would put aside today as a holiday gift to herself. Magda had laughed scornfully at her whimsy when she'd quietly come to help her dress that morning. Catherine would not be deterred. It was a real Christmas, the kind she'd dreamed of as a little girl, and she would embrace it fully no matter what cynicisms Magda threw her way.

"What are you thinking?" Giles asked, coming down the stairs to join her. "You were miles away just now." He grabbed up their cloaks and mufflers from a bench.

She shook her head. "Nothing. Everything." She turned to let Giles drape her riding cloak about her shoulders, liking the brush of his hands on her shoulders as he fitted the cape across them. "I've never had a proper Christmas. I suppose I am excited."

Giles laughed. "I hope Spelthorne lives up to your expectations then."

She smiled up at him. "How could it not with you in charge of everything? I bet even the mistletoe grows according to your plans."

"Let's go find out." Giles held out his hand for her and she took it, letting him lead her outside into the waiting throng of merrymakers who were eager to be off.

In the stableyard, Cate clapped her hands at the sight of the converted wagon that would convey them out to the Spelthorne woods. The wheels had been replaced with runners to glide over the snow. The empty wagon box would serve to carry back the greenery to the abbey later. Two draft horses had been harnessed with sleigh bells that jingled in the crisp air.

"Your chariot, madam. I am glad you're pleased," Giles said softly beside her before boosting her onto the wagon bench where she'd ride beside him as he drove the team.

The villagers and tenant farmers mounted up on similar converted wagons. Many piled into wagon boxes as if the outing were a hayride without the hay. Giles clucked to his team and they were off, forming a little parade. Those who had stayed behind to see to baking and last minute preparations waved to them from the cottages. Someone started a lively song, and soon the sound of merry voices joined the jingle of harness bells.

It was a beautiful day, a perfect day complete with a brilliant-blue winter sky overhead and sparkling white snow on the ground. The singers breaths came in great puffs as they sang. She could ask for no better setting against which to see her first Christmas unfold. She thought of the small gifts she had for Giles later and hoped they would be enough to convey how thankful she was for this day.

The sleigh-wagons pulled into a clearing and everyone piled out. Everyone knew their job from years of tradition. It was easy for Cate to fit into their rhythm.

The women took baskets and gathered holly full of berries, the leaves a waxy green against the snow. They hunted for mistletoe and other greens for the kissing bough they'd make back at the abbey.

The men set to work gathering great swags of greenery to decorate the mantle and to twist into a garland to drape down the long staircase. Another group of men,

led by Giles, took out axes and saws and set out to find
the perfect yule log.

Deep in the woods she could hear the men calling
out to one another and finally a victorious cry that the
right tree had been found. The women put down their
baskets and moved towards the voices, excitement rising at the prospect of seeing the yule log cut.

Cate joined the other women. She stared in amazement at what the men had found. It wasn't a log at all
by any stretch of her imagination. It was practically a
tree. She'd privately thought the men a bit ridiculous in
hauling out their saws but she could see now that a saw
would be put to good use.

The butcher and the blacksmith started the process of
cutting the great trunk into a log that could be hauled
back to the abbey. There were good-natured catcalls and
jests as their tremendous efforts resulted in little progress
on the trunk but plenty of sweat on their brows. After
awhile another team took over and another until all the
men in attendance had played a role in cutting the yule
log. Giles and the head groom from the abbey went last,
either by design or by accident, Cate wasn't sure which.

The day was cold but sawing was hot work. Giles
had shucked off his outerwear and rolled up the sleeves
of his shirt. Patches of sweat showed through the mate-
rial as he flexed and pushed with the saw, reminding all
present of the excellent physique of their earl.

At last Giles and the groom were triumphant. A great
cheer went up as the saw cut clean through for the final
time. There was much backslapping among the men

surrounding Giles and then ropes were lashed about the log, which was still much larger than she had expected. The men took up their places at the ropes and began the haul back to the wagons.

It was afternoon by the time the log was hitched to a team of horses and the wagons loaded with people and greenery. The afternoon was graying with the promise of more snow. People were cold and the prospect of hot drinks back at the abbey kept spirits high as they headed home.

Giles's housekeeper had mulled wine and hot sticky buns waiting for the glad crowd. The older participants drank for warmth and headed home for other preparations. The younger people stayed on to help with decorations.

In what seemed an impossibly short time, the abbey was transformed into a Christmas dream. Evergreen garlands draped around the banister of the staircase, adorned with bows Giles had brought down from the attic, saved from holidays past. The yule log was positioned in the large fireplace awaiting the night's festivities. The dining room had been prepared for the laying out of the abbey's silver and the Christmas feast. Spelthorne held nothing back. Tonight it would be silver and candles and plenty for all who attended.

As dusk fell, the young people sang out their goodbyes with promises to see each other shortly. Cate stood in the hall, watching the last of them go.

"There's one more thing to do," Giles said, materializing beside her.

"I can't imagine what that would be. We've done so much already," she said.

"It's down at the chapel. Are you up for a walk?" Giles took a lantern in one hand and her arm in another and led the way to the little chapel. There was no one there. It was quiet and dark and peaceful.

Giles set about lighting a few more candles. "We need to unpack that box in the corner." He nodded his head to large carton set near the altar. "I had it brought down earlier today."

"What is it?" Cate asked, going to the crate and opening it. She took out the wrapped pieces inside.

"Go ahead, unwrap them. Can't you guess?" Giles's voice was soft, almost reverent, causing her to wonder what could be so significant about the box.

She carefully unwrapped the first piece. She gave a little gasp. "Oh, it's a shepherd." She held the piece up to the flickering lights. "It's beautiful."

"It's a crèche, hand carved and painted from Italy. It was given to Celeste as a wedding gift from her father. She had a passion for Italian things," Giles said, coming to stand by Catherine.

"A crèche?" She tried the unfamiliar word out on her tongue as she unwrapped another piece.

"A nativity scene, a manger scene."

"Yes. I remember seeing one in a church." Cate took out a carved wise man wearing brilliant robes of blue and gold. "I don't think I have seen anything so lovely." She was about to ask why such a lovely, valuable thing was not kept on display at the abbey where it could be safeguarded but she already knew the answer. Putting this out on display for all to enjoy over the twelve days of Christmas was Spelthorne's gift to its people. This didn't belong to one man but to all of them, perhaps as much a part of Spelthorne's legacy as the land itself. Giles would never keep such a thing to himself.

They set the nativity up on the altar, carefully arranging all the pieces to their best advantage, talking a little as they did so.

"Did you never go to church on Christmas, Cate?" Giles asked hesitantly, setting up a cluster of sheep near the shepherds.

"No. No one wants gypsies in church," she said candidly. "Christmas was a lonely holiday for us. We had a little celebration of our own, perhaps eating meat or some extra ration of food to commemorate the day. It was a hard day in the heart of winter."

"I'm sorry," Giles offered quietly. "I didn't mean to pry or to bring up painful memories." There was an awkward pause. "Do you blame me for it?"

The question took her off-guard. "What do you mean?"

"Do you resent me because your life was so difficult?" The strong man who had sawed through the yule log, who'd effortlessly organized the activities of the day without error seemed momentarily vulnerable in the candlelight as he asked his question. "I have often wondered if you hold me to blame."

She shook her head. "No. None of that was a coil of your making. You were simply involved through no

knowledge or choice of your own. I do not resent you."
She reached out a hand to stroke his handsome face.
She wanted to dare more. In this moment it felt right to
say the words "I love you," to let him know that she saw
only the future when she thought of him, not the tumul-
tuous past which had dealt unfairly with them both. But
she could not bring the words to her lips so they stayed
silent in her heart, giving way to the caution that said
"not yet, not yet."

The night had been a splendid mixture of the boister-
ous and serene. The abbey had been filled with merrymakers drinking Bishop and Purl and eating roasted
turkey from the groaning table in the dining room. Near
midnight, she and Giles led a peaceful candlelight pro-
cession down to the chapel for Christmas services, then
caroled softly on the late walk home amid delicately
falling snowflakes.

Tucked away in the privacy of their chambers, they
took a moment's peace to sip a final mug of Bishop and
enjoy the quiet by the fire. Giles produced a small,
square, blue velvet box. "I had thought to wait until tomorrow, but this seems like the right moment to give
you this."

Cate took the soft case, caressing the velvet. "It's a
lovely box. Thank you." She would find something special to put in this box. "I have something for you too."
She rose but Giles stayed her with a gentle gesture.

"Wait. Open the box. There's something inside it."

"Oh." She sat back down, feeling slightly foolish. The

box was lavish enough to be a gift by itself. She opened the lid and found herself speechless. Bedded on blue satin that matched the velvet lay a single strand of pearls, all the same size and flawlessly white. "Oh, Giles, they're beautiful. This is a magnificent gift," she said in awe.

"Let me help you put them on." Giles came to her side and lifted the pearls from their bed. Deftly he slipped open the clasp and placed the necklace about her neck. She could feel them laying lightly against her skin. She lifted a finger to fondle them. "I've never worn anything so splendid."

"You'll wear all sorts of jewels in London," Giles said. "The Spelthorne vaults are there with the family jewels. I thought you might like something simpler to wear for every day while you're here."

Cate laughed nervously. "I can hardly imagine pearls being simple everyday jewels."

Giles covered her hand with his. "They look well on you, but anything would. You're a beautiful woman, Cate, no matter what you wear. I was proud to have you by my side today and tonight," he said quietly with such sincerity that she could not doubt the truth of what he spoke.

She cast her eyes down, undone by the compliment. "I hope you will be proud in London. I do not think London will be as easily conquered as Spelthorne. Everyone here has been so accepting, so kind. I do not think London will be as willing to embrace me."

Giles stroked the back of her hand. "Why wouldn't London fall in love with you as the people of Spelthorne have? As I have?"

She looked up at that. They had never mentioned love, but the expression in his eyes suggested he meant every word. "You've fallen in love with me?"

She was rewarded with a blush from Giles. He looked away briefly. *Was this self-confident man who effortlessly mastered crowds embarrassed by a single woman?* She could hardly believe it could be so until she thought of her own reticence in the chapel earlier.

He gave a small self-deprecating chuckle and continued to stare into the fire. "I have long thought that I was above voicing such sentimental drivel but apparently I am not." He cocked his head to catch a sideways glance of her. She offered an encouraging smile, urging him to continue, letting him know his sentiments were safe with her.

"When I look back, I think I began loving you the moment I saw you at the Denbigh's party. I feel like an infatuated school boy for saying it."

"We hardly talked except for business!" she exclaimed.

Giles shrugged. "I remember every moment. We sat on a low bench by the gate in the cold winter shrubbery. You held my hand and promised me a grand passion. I wished at the time that the grand passion would be you." He adjusted his position to face her squarely now, crouching on his haunches. He dropped his voice, and Cate leaned forward to listen. "I often regret not following my heart that night."

She held her breath, her eyes not daring to leave his blue gaze. His eyes smouldered now, desire coming to life as he made his confession. His hand drifted up to her hair and he continued his seduction, slowly plucking out the pins from her coiffure as he spoke.

"That night, I wanted to run my hands through your hair. It looked to me like silk. I find now that my impression was right." The feel of his hands combing through her hair, letting its length sift through his hands was intoxicating. "I wanted to know you." He drew his thumb lightly across her lips. "You seemed to me the epitome of goodness and perhaps freedom, a freedom I wanted for myself. I thought with you, I could be free."

"And are you?"

Giles buried his head in her lap. "Absolutely. Can you not see how you've changed me, Cate? You've made the most ordinary, extraordinary again. I like to see the world through your eyes; I like to show you new things, give you new experiences. You are my adventure, my grand passion. I am completely in your thrall."

He lifted his head, and she could not hide from him the tears that glistened in her eyes. She had not expected such a confession from him, ever. She'd conditioned herself not to think of such an impossibility. She'd accustomed herself to knowing that any deep affection would be on her side alone.

Giles reached up a hand to catch a tear drop. "Why do you cry?"

She sniffed. "Because I had not expected you to love me and because I have loved you for what seems like forever, only I was too frightened to say the words."

Giles drew her down to him. "Then we are agreed.

We are in love." He kissed her tenderly and she clung to him, wanting this moment to last all night.

They stayed by the fire for a long while, unwilling to let go of the quiet moment. It wasn't until later, when the fire had finally died down to mere embers that she realized she'd forgotten to give him her small gifts.

Giles laughed at her as she sprang up to get them. "They'll keep until morning," he said, drawing her tight against him. He nuzzled her neck. "Besides, I have the greatest gift of all tonight. I have your heart and you have mine. No gift or pearls can equal that, no matter how sincerely intended."

Cate turned in his arms. "Merry Christmas, husband."

Giles smiled in the darkness. "Merry Christmas, wife. I love you."

Cate held those words close to her heart, hoping he wouldn't regret them when they got to London.

Chapter Fifteen

London, end of January, 1819

In spite of her misgivings over going up to London, the day of departure arrived with alarming speed.

The Christmas holiday, accompanied by Twelfth-Night festivities and the New Year, had sped past in a bright kaleidoscope of parties and games. Christmas day Giles had opened the abbey to all for rowdy games of Blind Man's Bluff and other entertainments. In the days following, there'd been card parties in the village and an assembly dance in the upper rooms of the inn for New Year's.

She and Giles were invited everywhere. Everyone was thrilled to have the earl and his bride with them for so long. Cate was not surprised to learn that after discharging his holiday duties, Giles usually returned to the capitol as soon as possible. This year he lingered.

She suspected it was to give her as much time as he could to prepare herself for London. She also suspected that he wanted to postpone the trip as well.

She waited nervously in the entry hall for Giles to tell her the covered traveling coach had been loaded. All of their trunks had been brought down earlier to be placed in the luggage coach. She thought of the house party in the fall when she'd watched all the guests and their extraordinary piles of luggage, thinking how fantastical it was to have two conveyances. Then she'd hardly owned enough to fill a small trunk and she'd been wearing borrowed clothing. It was difficult to believe that had been only a few months ago; it seemed like a lifetime away.

She spotted Magda in the doorway of the drawing room. Even Magda looked respectable these days, dressed in a dark-blue wool gown appropriate to the status of a companion-cum-maid. With her iron-colored hair pulled back in a severe bun, no one would guess she'd been a gypsy fortune-teller a season ago. These days the woman looked every inch the formidable companion, although Magda was often left to her own devices since Catherine was spending more and more time with Giles.

"Magda, just look at us. Who would have thought?" Cate held out the skirt of her green traveling ensemble and made a small pirouette.

Magda nodded solemnly. "We've done well so far. This has turned out nicely but I don't like him taking you to London without me." She'd not quite gotten over her anger at Giles having Cate Dupeski's name on the marriage certificate.

Cate laughed lightly at Magda's fears. "Whyever not? Giles is perfectly capable of defending me if it comes to that." She desperately hoped it wouldn't.

"I am sure he is. He will defend you, even if it's only to ensure his own honor. He gains nothing from having you exposed."

"Speak plainly, Magda. I'm worried enough about this visit to town without you adding to it," Catherine scolded.

"Who will protect you from him?"

"That's nonsense, Magda. There's no need to be protected from him. He loves me, and I love him," Cate said simply.

Magda smirked at that. "Is that what he's been telling you these days? It's talk of love that's lit up your face? Be careful then. When love clouds the picture, you never see trouble coming until its too late."

"Are you ready, love?" Giles entered the foyer, riding gloves and traveling cape in hand. He shot Magda a pointed look that suggested he guessed the tenor of her conversation and highly disapproved.

Cate went to him, letting him drape her cloak about her shoulders. She could do without Magda's doubt. She had enough of her own. The last thing she needed was to doubt Giles. His support was the bulwark she was counting on to weather London and whatever storms it might throw her way.

The roads were jouncy affairs, rutted with frozen mud and icy clots of snow. Cate was thankful Spelthorne was so close to town. One slow day of progress was enough to see them up to the steps of Giles's townhouse an hour after dark. In the summer, the journey was a half-day at worst, but in the cold of winter with questionable roads that could break a horse's leg, it took double the time.

The townhouse was ready for them. Lights blazed in the windows and the steps had been shoveled free of snow. Inside, the butler, a starchy fellow called Robards, met them with dignity and presented the staff. Cate congratulated herself on being ready for that. She'd learned enough from Isabella's lessons and her own experiences at Spelthorne to be prepared to manage the staff. She smiled and nodded, doing her best to commit names to memory.

She'd lived with Giles long enough to expect elegance at every turn. But still, the townhouse was an opulent show-piece that exceeded the elegance of the abbey. Each room was a new discovery, done up in its own theme. The drawing room was done in the Egyptian style, the dining room done in the French style, all gilt and lightness. Giles's private office held pieces from the Far East.

The tour of the house was overwhelming. She was relieved to open the doors to their private chambers and find the décor in there greatly resembled the master chamber at the abbey. "Ah, we're home," she said, running a hand over the counterpane on the carved four-poster bed.

"That's exactly how I feel when I enter this room. This room is most like the abbey. There are no pretensions, just comfort." Giles encircled her waist with his arm and pulled her against him. "Will you be comfortable here?"

She leaned her back into him, feeling the warmth of his body. "I am comfortable wherever you are."

"I will try and not be gone too often," Giles offered, but she could sense it was a halfhearted remark since he could not possibly keep the promise.

She tried to assuage his worry. "I know. We talked about this in the carriage. I understand you have obligations in parliament. That is why we are here. I will be on my own many nights. I don't expect you to shirk your duties."

"Isabella and Tristan are in town. I noticed they'd already left a card downstairs. Isabella will take you around while Tristan and I are in session. You'll have a circle of friends and plenty of activities in no time if I know Isabella."

Cate knew he meant to be reassuring, but the mention of Tristan and Isabella wasn't all that comforting. "I know you mean well, Giles. But you mustn't force them to befriend me if they don't like me."

She hadn't seen Isabella since the wedding, and she wasn't certain that Isabella was ready to forgive her for the situation she'd placed Giles in. She knew Tristan wasn't. He'd been surprised by the announcement to wed, and he'd been firmly against Giles's decision even though he'd supplied the roses for the ceremony.

Giles hugged her in reassurance. "They will like you. Once they see that we have grown an honest affection for one another and that we've put the past behind us, they will accept you on your own merit."

Giles's predictions proved to be true almost immediately. The next morning, Isabella took Cate shopping, beginning the elaborate process of constructing a town wardrobe. In the afternoon, she accompanied Isabella to a ladies' tea. That evening she and Isabella went to a musicale hosted by one of Isabella's friends while Tristan and Giles sat in parliament.

That became the pattern of their days. Giles was busy although when he was home, Cate would sit in his private office with him, quietly stitching or reading while he read papers and proposed legislation.

"You must be looking forward to such a grand occasion as the Rosamund Ball tonight," Giles said one day as they spent a rare lunch together. "Everything you've attended so far has been small gatherings with Isabella. She says you've taken well."

"I daresay a ball and a musicale are two different things." Cate worried the fabric of her skirt, pleating it between her fingers, anxiety evident on her face.

Giles rose and crossed the distance between them, wanting to alleviate her anxiety. He knelt beside her and stopped her fidgeting hands with his own. "They aren't that different."

"Not to you. You were born to such things. How to con-duct yourself is as commonplace to you as breathing." Cate sighed. "At a musicale, all I have to do is sit next to Isabella, balance a plate of cake and a teacup on my lap and smile while she does all the talking. I nod in the right places, of course." She added the last with a bit of teasing.

Giles laughed. "You've done well. You'll do well to-night. I'll be there and I won't let anything happen to you." He'd said it in good humor but ballrooms were nothing short of social battlefields.

"Is it so dire as all that? Will I truly need protection?"

"Of course not. But balls are bigger occasions than musicales. Up until now, there has not been enough peo-ple in town for anyone to pull off a ball, but now that the politicians have come flooding back in, more and more families are arriving every day. The Rosamunds think they have their two hundred."

"Two hundred?" Cate's eyes widened in astonish-ment. "Two hundred what?"

"Two hundred guests. The *ton* matrons have ruled that one must invite at least two hundred guests for an event to qualify as a ball."

"I can't imagine putting two hundred people in a home the size of this one."

Giles tapped her on the nose. "That's why they call it a 'crush.' "

She began laughing and after that Giles found he could not pay attention to his papers. He gave up and spent the afternoon answering Cate's questions about balls and how to go on. Society was a silly thing he discovered as he explained all its intricacies to his wife. No wonder Tristan and Isabella preferred time in the country to town. He was starting to feel the same way, especially when Cate asked a question regarding form that he had no ready answer for.

They laughed away the afternoon in companionable camaraderie, her head resting in his lap as they lounged on the settee. Giles thought he'd never spent a better set of hours, as he ran a lazy hand through the black spread of her hair falling over his leg.

He hoped he'd appeased her fears, although he could not say they were unfounded. He'd laughed her concerns away but they were his concerns as well. What would the *ton* think of his hasty marriage? Would anyone care enough to make a scandal out of it? To discover the murky depths of *DeBrett's* and *Burke's* offered no answer to who his bride was, only more mystery?

He hadn't said anything to her, but he was worried. With more people coming up to town all the time, it was inevitable they would encounter guests from his house party who recalled his cousin, Catherine Winthrop. He and Cate maintained that identity. In public she was called Catherine. Isabella had introduced her as Catherine. There was little harm in it, if she went by Catherine or Cate. It was essentially the same name.

But those questions would come. He could explain away her lack of placement in *Debrett's* with the simple claim that she was too far removed for such notice. There would only be trouble if someone saw the marriage certificate, but that was sealed in the parish records.

Someone would have to want to find out and go hunting for it.

He found that he didn't care if anyone questioned her origins but he did care very deeply if those questions hurt her.

Tristan and Isabella called for them promptly at 7:00, having decided that it would be best if all four of them arrived together. After all, Isabella had actively behaved as Cate's sponsor since her arrival in London, and Giles and Tristan had a long-standing friendship. For them to be together was only natural and shouldn't denote anything beyond their commonly acknowledged friendship; only the Greshams and Giles knew that it had been arranged as a stratagem to promote and, if necessary, to protect Cate.

"Are you ready, old friend?" Tristan asked, watching his wife mount the staircase to check on Cate.

Giles gave a somber nod. "Yes. She's worried of course. She's afraid she'll let me down. I could care less." He turned to face Tristan. "I worry about her being hurt, by someone saying a cruel thing or making insinuations."

Tristan knitted his brow. "She's lived on the outside of society, suffered great verbal insult in her lifetime. I doubt the barbs of our dragons could do her serious injury. Your wife is no shrinking violet."

Giles chuckled a bit at that. Tristan was right. He'd spent too long thinking of her as his wife, his responsibility, that he often forgot she was capable of looking after herself. "It's hard for me to remember that sometimes. Still, it's not the dragons I worry about. It's the questions that might be asked, and worse yet the answers that might be uncovered. I worry for her, I worry for Spelthorne."

Tristan put a comforting hand on Giles's shoulder. "Let them ask their questions, Giles. We've done our jobs well. If anyone comes looking, they won't find the answers." His eyes shifted to a point over Giles's shoulder. "God, she's beautiful."

Giles turned. Their wives stood on the stairs, arm in arm as they began their descent. It never occurred to Giles that perhaps Tristan's comment had referred to Isabella, who was exquisitely turned out in her trademark copper silk. It was Cate who held all his attention. The hours her maid had spent with her in preparation for the evening had created a vision that was heretofore unequaled in Giles's opinion.

Dressed in an aquamarine gown of fine Norwich bombazine, she was the image of chic beauty. Everything about the gown from the gored ankle-length skirts scalloped at the hem to show off the cream silk underskirt beneath to the elegant drape of the Spanish slashing of the sleeves, her attire was the first stare of fashion. No one could gainsay the quality of her wardrobe. More than that, she carried it off with ease.

Giles recognized immediately that it was not so much the dress that transformed her, but that she'd transformed the dress. Her dark hair was an excellent foil for the aquamarine tones of the fabric, and in turn, the gown showed off the sparkle of her green eyes to their best advantage.

In her wake, Isabella, who'd always been the standard against which Giles weighed other English beauties, seemed less extraordinary.

Giles handed his wife into the carriage, whispering to her as she moved passed him, "You look wonderful."

The line into the Rosamund's mansion was long by the time the carriage pulled up to let them out. Giles had planned it that way. The longer the line, the more likely that dancing would have started before they were announced. People would be engaged in their dancing and in their own social sets. They would already have had plenty of time to look around and see who was there and less likely to single him out.

Not that he minded being singled out. He was not a coward and felt confident in holding his own with anyone. But he wanted to make the evening as enjoyable as possible for Cate, who fairly bristled with tension beside him. He recognized that in part some of her nerves were generated by excitement over attending a ton ball. But part of them was also generated over her concern about the unknown. How would she be received?

Giles squeezed her hand as they joined the queue of guests with Tristan and Isabella. He bent his head to find her ear. "Everything will be fine. There is this world of theirs and there is the world we've created for ourselves. There is nothing they can say or do that can penetrate what we've built between us, my love."

Cate smile at Giles's words. She wanted to believe him. But she'd lived a cynical life too long to accept that anything could be that easy. Still, she did her best to enjoy the evening. There was plenty to enjoy.

After the receiving line, they made their way to the ballroom and its lavish decorations. Cate had never seen such floral luxury in the middle of winter. The ballroom looked and smelled like a hothouse. Every niche was filled with huge urns full of roses of varying colors and wintergreens. Candles blazed from two one hundred candle chandeliers hanging over the expanse of the ballroom. At the far end in a balcony overlooking the ballroom, the five piece orchestra was already playing.

"It's fantastical," she breathed.

"That's exactly the right word for it," Tristan grimaced, steering Isabella into a clear space as they moved forward. "I can't imagine what it took to force so many roses into bloom this time of year."

Isabella poked him with an elbow. "It's still lovely to look at. I like it. I am reminded that after a dreary winter spring can't be far away."

The orchestra struck up a waltz. "Will you dance with me, Catherine, while these two argue about the merits of roses in winter?" Giles asked, careful to use the right name.

Cate let him sweep her into the sea of dancers, appreciating the firm hand he kept at the small of her back. She let him set the tone and fell into rhythm with him easily, having learned her lessons well since the first time they'd danced together.

"One of the best aspects of being married is that now I can dance with you as much as I wish," Giles confided as they took the high turn. "I am no longer limited to two miserly dances a night."

She gave a flirting smile. "I thought . . ." She paused in mid-sentence. "Oh dear."

She forced Giles to turn her so he could see too. Swirling towards them in a cloud of figured periwinkle satin was Lady Fox-Haughton in the arms of a handsome Norse god. There was no pretending she didn't see them.

Giles met them with a polite nod as the two couples twirled past each other. "It was bound to happen at some point," he said to Cate once the couples had cleared the dance floor and they could rejoin Isabella and Tristan.

"Perhaps that's all we'll see of them," Cate said hopefully, although she didn't believe it. That woman had been far too possessive of Giles to simply give him up. If she had been angry about his attentions to a shirt-tail relative in the fall, she'd be livid about his having married the relative instead of making no attempt to win back her favor.

"You've seen them, then?" Isabella was saying. "She has a new amour now, Alistair Manley, an earl's third son."

"He's fairly young and just newly come to town. His father has set him up as an MP for one of the rotten boroughs under his control," Tristan put in, distaste for the man's acquisition of power evident in his tone.

"I don't believe I know him," Giles said idly.

Cate watched Isabella lift her eyebrows and feared the worst. "It seems, Giles, that will soon be remedied. They're headed this way."

Giles squared his shoulders and Cate felt him increase the intensity of his grip on her hand. She drew herself up as well. If there was to be a reckoning, Giles would not be alone.

"Good evening, Spelthorne." Lady Fox-Haughton extended her hand although her tones were cool. "I'd heard you brought your new wife up to town." She cast her eyes on Cate and gave her a full study. "I wonder what other surprises you have for us, Spelthorne?"

The comment was not even couched in the barest of disguises. Cate felt her temper rise at the insinuation that Giles had married her for the sake of an ill-conceived child, hatched in passion without the blessing of matrimony.

Giles made a gallant gesture of raising her gloved hand to his lips and kissing it before tucking it back into the crook of his arm. "The only surprise is love. It is hard to know when Cupid's dart will find its mark. But when it does, its aim is true."

The rejoinder was well done. Cate recognized at once that there was nothing the woman could say without well-wishing them unless she wanted to appear catty.

Still, Lady Fox-Haughton was not a master of her craft because she gave up easily. "Happiness can be found in many strange places. However this is the first time I've heard of it being found beyond the grave."

"I am not certain at all as to what you mean," Giles said.

Lady Fox-Haughton turned to the man beside her. "Tell him what you've discovered."

The blond man leered at Cate while addressing Giles. "There is no Catherine Winthrop. A fourth cousin by that name died in infancy. Your bride doesn't exist."

"This fellow is charming, Candice." Giles turned the full force of his blue gaze on the woman. "It is plainly visible to all that my bride exists. She stands here right now."

"She's not Catherine Winthrop," Lady Fox-Haughton protested, her voice rising enough to attract the attention of those around them.

"Then who is she?" Giles challenged, wanting to end this nonsense before the entire ballroom was alerted.

"She's a fraud. She's either duped you or you've conspired with her to pass her off as a shirttail relative for some dark reason."

That did it. The scene Giles wanted to avoid now held center stage among London's finest. The ballroom was silent, waiting for his response. Beside him, Tristan was alert and rigid but there was nothing his friend could do.

"Your accusations are outlandish, foolish, and entirely unsubstantiated," Giles said, holding Alistair's gaze evenly. The man needed to have one last chance to back down.

"No, they are not," Lady Fox-Haughton said in a quiet tone that was far more menacing than the loud accusations. With an imperial gesture of her hand, she beckoned to someone at the back of the ballroom. The crowd parted and a severely dressed woman of middle years walked to Candice's side.

It was Magda.

Cate felt weak. She clung to Giles's arm for support. All that she feared would happen now. Her world would come crashing down. Giles would never forgive her for this.

"I believe you know this woman?" Candice said.

"She works at the abbey as a companion to my wife," Giles returned coldly, his mind working quickly to ascertain the twists and turns of Candice's arguments. *What direction would she go? How much did she know? How much truth would have to be told to extricate Cate from Candice's web of revenge.*

Candice raised her voice to assure being heard. "Before she was a 'companion,' she was your wife's foster mother when they lived together with a gypsy caravan."

The crowd aahed over this bit of information, their speculations rising in volume.

"This is an interesting low you've sunk to, Spelthorne," Manley drawled, relishing the moment. "You're always so perfect, so above reproach and now you've been caught married to a gypsy whore whom you've tried to pass off as a distant relation."

Giles's fist met with the side of Manley's jaw. Manley staggered backward, falling into the crush of people who'd gathered to hear what was sure to be tomorrow's juiciest *on-dit.*

Cate gave a little scream but Giles didn't care. Manley's comments were beyond the pale no matter what the truth of the accusations. No one spoke about his wife in such terms. He leapt after Manley's staggering form and tackled the man to the ground.

Excited screams broke out from the ladies and men began laying side wagers. Giles landed three successive blows before Manley pushed him off and regained his feet.

The fight evened out then. Taller than Giles and outweighing him by two stone, Manley managed a jab to the stomach that had Giles reeling against the wall. The man hung back, breathing hard and gathering himself before launching another attack. "I wonder, Spelthorne, did you know what she was or were you the complete cuckold?"

Giles lowered his head, his temper racing, and prepared to charge the blond giant. Only Magda's ill-timed words stayed his mad rampage.

"Oh, he knew." Magda's voice stopped the brawl. "The perfect earl knew. He married her to save Spelthorne and his miserable pride."

"No, Magda. Stop this!" Cate cried out from Isabella's side.

Magda whirled on her. "You're the rightful heir to the title. He married you to silence your claims. I have given you a chance to take back what is yours. Once you're free of his seductions, you'll thank me for this."

The guests fell on the information like hungry wolves to meat. The volume in the ballroom soared to a roar only to be quieted by Manley's jeering question. "If Moncrief isn't Spelthorne, then who is he?"

"A cottager's son," Magda said resolutely.

Horrified, Cate turned to Tristan. "You're his friend, do something! Get us out of here." If this went on any longer, Manley and Giles would beat each other to a bloody pulp and that would just be the start of it. Giles's sense of honor would demand a duel, and she couldn't bear the risk of losing him.

Tristan stepped between Manley and Giles. "Gentlemen, there's much that should be discussed before this goes any farther. Please retreat. Lady Rosamund, my apologies on their behalf." Tristan put an arm about Giles's shoulders and ushered him from the room before anyone could protest. Catherine and Isabella followed discreetly behind.

Lady Rosamund had offered them a private room, but Tristan refused and bundled the group into the carriage, not wanting to give Lady Rosamund any more gossip for the mill. Her ball would be the talk of the town tomorrow morning as it was.

"I will see that woman in hell," Giles was still angry an hour later as he sat in his library, a cold rag over the swelling bruise on his cheek.

"Which one?" Tristan asked wryly, helping himself to a glass of whiskey from the sideboard.

"Both of them I suppose." Giles sat up. "I can't believe Candice sent Manley to Spelthorne and convinced Magda to talk."

Cate sat in a corner by the fire, feeling miserable. Magda's revelations had made Giles look like a liar. He'd known, he'd devised the deception, trading his name in marriage for the silencing of her claims.

"This is all my fault," Cate said, stricken and lonely in her corner.

Giles looked her way. "No, it isn't. It's mine for even thinking such a scandal could be avoided. I was foolish to try to cover it up as if no one would find out. It was not well done of me."

Tristan cut through the melancholy. "Nonetheless, what is done is done. The news will be all over London tomorrow. We must move quickly to secure Spelthorne in case the crown decides Spelthorne should revert to royal jurisdiction in the absence of an obvious heir, or perhaps decides Spelthorne should go to another male relative with an unspoiled bloodline."

He gave Cate a hard look. "You need to decide where your loyalties are. Will you cast your lot with Magda in an attempt to secure your legacy or will you stand by your husband?"

Cate rose, anger flaring in her green eyes, fists clenched at her sides. "You should not even have to ask. I am for Giles."

"Tristan," Giles spoke sternly. "This is not her fault. She's not to blame. I will not tolerate such insinuations against her, even from a friend," he warned.

Cate warmed a little at Giles's defense.

Giles put down the rag and sat forward. "I have a plan to secure Spelthorne. The circumstances are not as dire as they seem at the moment."

It was a difficult week. Gossip surrounded them ranging from speculation about Giles's birth to questions about Catherine Winthrop's gypsy origins. But cool heads prevailed.

Giles's plan was a good one, using the very marriage certificate and name in question that had begun Lady Fox-Haughton's accusations. Best of all, it muddled the importance of even determining the legitimate heir to the Spelthorne title. If the heir was indeed Giles's wife, then all that she had legally reverted to her husband upon her marriage, still making Giles the legally recognized holder of the title. If not, the signature of the bride hardly mattered. Giles Moncrief could marry whomever he liked. After all, hadn't his friend Baron Wickham married a French citizen?

The solution was met favorably in the circles that mattered. In royal circles, the prince-regent was only too glad to have the matter resolved swiftly without having to be involved in any legal inquiries. Giles was too valuable a voice in parliament to be risk losing.

With the prince-regent's endorsement, the residual gossip about Giles and his new bride turned them into a couple straight out of fairy tales until much had been forgotten, and much had been turned into instant romantic legend about the Moncriefs. Lady Fox-

Haughton had failed to ruin Giles socially by seeing his reputation falter under the scandal of his inheritance.

It was with a great sense of triumph and relief a week later that Tristan and Isabella rode with Giles and Cate in Hyde Park. Cate beamed at Giles's side as they greeted well-wishers.

"We've resolved it. You did it with your marvelous arguments and brains," Tristan congratulated Giles during a quiet moment.

"Thank you for standing by me, by us," Giles returned.

"Am I too late to toast your gypsy whore?" A voice belonging to Alistair Manley sneered from behind Giles's group on the path.

Giles wheeled his horse around to face Manley, feeling Tristan turn with him. "You are warned sirrah, to watch your words when they are directed at my wife."

"Do you think a title and pretty clothes can make people forget? A plow horse can never be a thoroughbred no matter who rides it."

Giles clenched his jaw against the coarse innuendo. "Have you come here to stir up more of Lady Fox-Haughton's trouble or do you come on your own accord?"

A few of the gathered bystanders chuckled at that. One of them called out, "He's got you there, Manley. You'd do better to have your own opinions and let hers go hang."

Manley's face reddened at the implications, and Giles saw that the banter had made the situation worse.

This man would not back down now and he would be the whipping boy for Manley's temper.

"Do you impugn my honor by suggesting I let a woman espouse my thoughts?" Manley said, flushed with temper and dismounting.

Giles followed suit, ready to swing a fist if need be.

"No one impugns your honor no more than you impugn mine in regards to my lady wife," Giles said steadily, knowing the big giant couldn't agree to one without agreeing to other. If he did, then Giles had a right to fight.

"I will not be likened to that woman," Manley growled.

That did it. Giles swung his fist in a neat motion and connected with Manley's jaw. Manley fell hard into an unconscious heap.

The crowd gasped and swarmed closer. Someone emerged to tend Manley but Giles was only aware of Cate at his side. He drew her to him, wanting to protect her, hating that she'd heard Manley's words.

"What was that for?" Cate asked.

"That was for you," Giles said in a low voice.

"Giles, you can't fight them all," Cate said softly. "Manley won't be the last to cast aspersions."

"No one calls my wife a whore," Giles said with quiet fortitude. "You're my Romany heiress." It was meant for Cate alone but those surrounding the odd scene heard it as well. A few of them burst into spontaneous applause. It was not often such romance played out in their cynical lives full of arranged marriages. This was one for the record books.

"I like that," Cate said, trying the phrase out. "Romany heiress it is."

Giles smiled at Cate and then couldn't resist. He bent and kissed her full on the mouth much to the approval of all who looked on.